MARCH OR DIE

Leo Kessler is a familiar name to readers of war fiction. In addition to his numerous superselling war series he is the author of several non-fiction works.

Also by Leo Kessler

The *SS Assault Regiment Wotan* Series

SS PANZER BATTALION
DEATH'S HEAD
CLAWS OF STEEL
GUNS AT CASSINO
THE DEVIL'S SHIELD
HAMMER OF THE GODS
FORCED MARCH
BLOOD AND ICE
THE SAND PANTHERS
COUNTER-ATTACK
PANZER HUNT
SLAUGHTER GROUND
HELLFIRE
FLASHPOINT
CAULDRON OF BLOOD
SCHIRMER'S HEADHUNTERS
WHORES OF WAR
SCHIRMER'S DEATH LEGION
SLAUGHTER AT SALERNO

The *Stormtroop* Series

STORMTROOP
BLOOD MOUNTAIN
VALLEY OF THE ASSASSINS
RED ASSAULT
HIMMLER'S GOLD
FIRE OVER KABUL
WAVE OF TERROR
EAGLES IN THE SNOW
FIRE OVER AFRICA

The *Rommel* Series

GHOST DIVISION
MASSACRE

The *Otto Stahl* Series

OTTO'S PHONEY WAR
OTTO'S BLITZKRIEG!
OTTO AND THE REDS
OTTO AND THE YANKS
OTTO AND THE SS
OTTO AND THE HIMMLER LOVE LETTERS

The *Sea Wolves* Series

SINK THE SCHARNHORST
DEATH TO THE DEUTSCHLAND

Also:

As Klaus Konrad

The *Russian* Series

FIRST BLOOD
MARCH ON MOSCOW
FRONT SWINE

LEO KESSLER

March or Die

Wotan 21

Futura

A Futura Book

First published in Great Britain in 1985
by Futura Publications, a Division of
Macdonald & Co (Publishers) Ltd
London & Sydney
and by Century Hutchinson Ltd in hardback

*All characters in this publication are fictitious
and any resemblance to real persons, living or dead,
is purely coincidental.*

ISBN 0 7088 2662 8

Printed and bound in Great Britain by
Collins, Glasgow

Futura Publications
A Division of
Macdonald & Co (Publishers) Ltd
Maxwell House
74 Worship Street
London EC2A 2EN

A BPCC plc Company

PROLOGUE

A Call to Arms

The sky was the colour of lead. The atmosphere was heavy and humid. In the pines the cigalas rasped harshly. Over the flat wash of the sea, the heat rippled in blue waves. All was tense expectation . . .

They had been waiting now for nearly three months for them to come, ever since June when the Anglo-Americans had landed in Normandy, dug in all along this burningly hot coast where before the war millionaires had taken their pleasure. For come they must. They would come from the sea, crack through the thin line of the defenders, and hurtle north to link up with their comrades in Normandy. Ever since Field Marshal Rommel had ordered the erection of the *Suedwall*, the South Wall, this whole French coastline had been the scene of furious activity. Every hotel, restaurant and private villa overlooking the sea had been bricked up and turned into a stronghold. Every inlet, beach and river mouth had been wired, mined and booby-trapped, and covered by machine-guns, anti-tank guns and flame throwers. For every kilometre there were three bunkers and a battery of heavy guns. Huge minefields had been planted everywhere, running right down to the beaches from the steep white cliffs.

But it was not only the coasts that had been fortified against the invaders. Behind the defenders, the hinterland had been prepared for the attack to come, too. Level stretches of countryside had been strewn with anti-tank obstacles, criss-crossed with steel wires to tear the wings off gliders and studded with sharpened stakes to impale unsuspecting paras. To a depth of twenty kilometres, in a line running from the Italian to the Spanish frontier, the whole of Southern France had been made ready for them . . .

And now they were coming. Intelligence had reported the massing of their armies in Italy. Air reconnaissance had spotted the invasion barges lining up in Corsica. The American fleet had been seen steaming through the Straits of Gibraltar. Churchill had vanished from the enemy capital, London, and everyone knew what that meant: *the drunken old sot was on his way to watch the invasion*!

Now on this sultry dawn of 15th August, 1944, they came in - at last. It started with what seemed the roar of an infuriated beast far out at sea, a dull groaning noise unlike anything else in the world. Like a hunting cry it echoed and re-echoed. Once, twice, three times, it roared. In their trenches and pill-boxes, the sweating, ashen-faced men tensed. Officers raised their hands to give the signal. NCOs pursed their lips over the whistles. In the command bunkers, staff officers hunched ready over their phones. Others poised, wide-eyed and fearful, over the alarm buttons.

A creaking like a badly tuned organ. Instinctively the snipers drew their rifles back from the parapets of their hides. The mortar crews hunched together like men caught in a sudden gale. Words of command froze on officers' lips. An eternity of oppressive silence. Far out at sea cherry-red lights flickered angrily. Still no sound. *Would it never begin*?

With a hoarse exultant scream, four hundred shells came hurtling in. In an instant that dread, tense silence had been broken as they slammed into the ground, making the very earth tremble under that awesome impact. The pre-landing bombardment had commenced and all hell was suddenly let loose . . .

Now the din was continuous and simultaneous. The thunder of the guns. The vicious scream of the overhead. The frenzied, hugely amplified staccato of the shell-burst to the front. Flames, gunpowder, pieces of copper as big as a fist, earth, sand, rock - *bodies*! Now this man-made cyclone crept steadily forward, up the beach, along the cliffs, stretching outwards to the land beyond, ripping apart all that lay in its path, submerging everything in that great, angry baleful scream that meant death. A horse running frantically along the sand, its mane afire. A cook dead and floating, a scalded pink, in his own soup kettle. A relief company, all polished boots and oiled rifles, neatly piled along the side of an approach road like sardines in a can, not a mark on them. A handless corporal trying to aid an officer both of whose legs were gory stumps, jetting scarlet blood into the sand. Dead and dying, flame and fury everywhere . . .

Now in the command bunkers the telephones jingled everywhere. Ashen-faced, wild-eyed staff officers ran back and forth. Dispatch riders sped away, bearing their tidings of woe and alarm. '*Rayol Plage taken . . . Enemy troops landing at Cap Negre . . . Barges off Cannes . . . Attack force making for St Tropez . . !*' The reports of the staff officers were mingled with the desperate cries for support, aid, orders. '*Flame-throwing attack in progress, bunker B . . . Can't stop them, hundreds of them attacking up the beach . . . Down to last five rounds . . . Request permission to withdraw . . . All officers save myself dead . . . what can I do . . . HEAVEN, ARSE AND CLOUDBURST . . . WHAT CAN I DO, SIR . . ?*'

To those of General Wiese's officers watching, there was something sinister yet majestic about the great air fleet that was now coming in to lead the attack on the German 19th Army's rear positions. The long line of bombers, which they knew stretched across the Mediterranean all the way back to Italy, twinkled like fairy lights in the ascending sun. To their front the pathfinders had already dropped their marker flares and were turning away in graceful curves for the journey back home. Now the flares dropped slowly in widening cascades like showers of jewels reluctant to obey the force of gravity. Already the flak had taken up the challenge. The sky was dotted with brown and grey puffs of exploding shells like a giant net through which the planes flew seemingly untouched. Now the canopies of the invading paras blossomed against the sullen, flecked sky. White, red, green, yellow, descending in their hundreds, their thousands. .

The gliders were being released, too. Great clumsy canvas and wood constructions, they came swooping down in frightening silence to discharge their cargoes of men and material. One hissed down an alley of cypress trees, sheered off both wings, and came to a shuddering, shivering halt like a projectile. Another hit a great oak, shattered, cartwheeled, and fell on its back like an upturned insect. No one got out. Some pilots tried to use the sharpened stakes which littered the fields around the HQ as brakes, hitting them at eighty kilometres an hour and slamming to a bone-shuddering stop in a great cloud of dust. Other pilots were not so lucky. They found their gliders impaled or torn apart by the steel wires. With crumpled wings, the shattered spars bulging out of the broken canvas fuselages, they lay in the fields like martyred birds.

But there was no stopping the paras and the gliderborne infantry. They were forming up everywhere, grabbing their equipment, loading the jeeps, streaming out of the littered fields beneath the canopies hanging from the trees, heading for the attack . . .

'They have landed the First Provisional Parachute Division, sir . . . Elements of the 36th and 45th American infantry divisions are also ashore, sir, beginning to push north. We have also learned that the French First . . .'

General Wiese, Commander of the German 19th, listened as if mesmerized as his Intelligence officer read the details from the clipboard. Outside the underground bunker he could hear the muffled thunder of the guns and the roar of aircraft. Inside, the hectic clatter of the teleprinters, the hurried to-and-fro of his staff and the incessant jingle of the field telephones told him, too, that time was running out for his army in southern France. The enemy had struck, as had long been expected, but in a strength he had not anticipated.

'In short, sir,' the bespectacled Intelligence man, who in civilian life had been a schoolteacher, concluded, 'we estimate that by zero twenty-three hundred hours tonight, the Anglo-Americans will have put some ninety to ninety-five thousand troops ashore.' He adjusted his pince-nez, cleared his throat, and looked down at the General's balding head, as if he were back in his provincial *Gymnasium* waiting for an answer from some particularly stupid boy.

Wiese took his time. He knew the High Command's contingency plan for the event of invasion. He was to hold as long as possible, but he was not to allow his army to get bogged down. The Führer did not think southern France important enough to waste an army there. The 19th had permission, when he thought necessary, to retreat up the length of France to the north where it would be used to support the great counter-stroke which would throw the Western Allies out of Normandy and back into the sea from whence they had come. Already in Berlin the staff were talking triumphantly of a second Dunkirk. Wiese stroked his chin thoughtfully, as if he were checking that he had shaved carefully enough this dawn, and said: 'What of the defences on the coast, Dietrich?'

The Intelligence officer consulted his clipboard once more. 'Patchy, sir,' he announced. 'Here and there our men are holding out against superhuman odds in a noble and heroic –'

Wiese waved a languid hand and said, as if bored, 'Enough of the heroics, Dietrich! Leave that to the Poison Dwarf* for home consumption. Just give me the facts, please.'

Dietrich flushed and hastily removed his pince-nez to rub the glass, hiding his nervousness in the same manner he had when the headmaster or some prowling, inquisitive inspector had visited his classroom. 'Both the 148th and 242nd Infantry Divisions have begun to retreat, or they were when we last heard from them.'

'*Last heard from them*?' Wiese sat up suddenly, his languid mood abruptly vanishing. 'What in three devils' name is that supposed to mean?'

Dietrich swallowed hard. 'All land-line and telephone contact with Ruffiac here' – he meant the site of the

* Nickname given to the vitriolic, dwarflike Minister of Propaganda, Dr Goebbels

headquarters – 'and the two divisional HQs went a quarter of an hour ago.'

Wiese slapped a hand to his high forehead like a man sorely tried, unable to react for a moment.

Across the big underground room, an officer with the purple stripe of the Greater General Staff running down the side of his overlarge riding breeches was staring at the telephone, breathing into it incredulously, '*But you can't mean that . . . you can't! A whole regiment surrendering . . . Absolut unmöglich*!'

'Resistance, those damned treacherous resistance people of the *maquis*,' Wiese exclaimed bitterly, finding his voice at last.

'We guess so, sir. Obviously the attack on our communications with the forward areas was coordinated to time with the landings.'

'So here am I,' Wiese moaned, 'like a chessplayer blindfolded and with his hands tied behind his damned back.' He pulled himself together with a visible effort of will. 'Von Bonin,' he called to the staff officer still frozen at the phone across the room. 'Give the signal for the mass of the Army to begin withdrawing. We have little time left. Those slant-eyed Turks, Georgians and Armenians of the 148th and 242nd won't hold the enemy very long. Just let's pray that they can do so long enough for us to get the rest of the Army moving northwards. At the double now!'

'*Jawohl, Herr General*!' the big, fat middle-aged staff officer barked as if he were an eighteen-year-old recruit. He began whirling the wheel of the field telephone furiously.

Wiese turned his attention back to the Intelligence officer. 'What of the *maquis* to our rear on the route march along the Rhône valley to Lyon and through the mountains to Grenoble?'

'Well, sir, in the mountains around Vercors, which used to be their main stronghold, they have become pretty tame ever since we dealt with them in June. If you recall –'

'I don't want to recall that particular massacre, Dietrich,'

Wiese interrupted him harshly. 'What of the resistance in the Rhône valley?'

'We can expect trouble in Lyon, perhaps in Valence too. Where there is industry there are communists, and where there are communists there is armed resistance.'

'In the name of God, man, *don't lecture me*! So, in short, both the main routes we shall take – the *Route Nationale* Seven to Lyon and the old *Route Napoleon* to Grenoble – are endangered? Am I correct in that?'

'Yessir.'

Across at the phone von Bonin was barking, 'I don't care whether you have an *Ami* poked right up your arse, Major, I am ordering you to move out straightaway! Fart hard and blow your way free, that's a direct order!' He snorted hard and, red-faced with anger, slammed the receiver down only to start whirling the handle yet again.

'What of the security forces? What have we got to take care of the *Route Napoleon*?' asked Wiese.

'Two battalions of stomachs and one of ears-and-noses.'*

Wiese nodded his approval. 'All good expendable cannon-fodder,' he said cynically. 'An *Ami* bullet will undoubtedly cure their afflictions one day soon. The *Route Nationale* Seven to Lyon?'

'The French, sir, just the French.'

'What kind of French?' Wiese rasped, his cynicism vanished. He knew just how shaky some of Germany's French allies had become since the June invasion of Normandy. They would go over to the enemy at the drop of a hat if it meant saving their precious skins.

'SS,' Dietrich answered promptly. 'A convalescent company of the French SS Division Charlemagne at Orange.'

'Good! At least they won't run over to the enemy.' Wiese chuckled sombrely. 'There's no hope for them. If they tried it, the French would slaughter them mercilessly.'

* In the Germany Army in WWII, unfit men with common afflictions such as bad stomachs were grouped together for treatment and in order to simplify their feeding. Hence 'stomach' and 'ears-and-nose' battalions

Dietrich frowned, as if he had suddenly remembered just how vulnerable all of them were, cut off from the bulk of the Germany Army by eight hundred kilometres of territory which had that day virtually become enemy country. 'And there is the Marchant Battalion of the *Milice*.'*

'Ah, I have heard of the celebrated *Commandant* Marchant and his police. They call him the Angel of Death, don't they?' Wiese smiled cynically again. 'Leaves his calling card in the form of his branded initials – "MM" – on each of his victims. A very pleasant chap indeed. I am quite sure that *he* won't go over to the enemy. Now what have we got in the way of German armour reserves? These French stubble-hoppers will have little more than rifles and machine-guns, I suspect. We must stiffen them with some armoured firepower to keep that damned road open.'

'SS Assault Regiment Wotan, sir,' Dietrich replied promptly, ears already taking in the sinister drone of heavy bombers – many of them – outside.

Wiese beamed. '*Himmelherrgott*!' he exclaimed with delight, eyes sparkling for the first time since the disaster which had overwhelmed his front had struck this dawn. 'Are you sure? I last heard of them on the Italian front. You say they are in the command area? Well, speak up, man!'**

'They took a bad beating at Cassino, were reinforced with new men from the South Tyrol, and were on their way to the Normandy front when they got held up at Grenoble.'

'Have they got armour?' Wiese asked hurriedly, for he too could hear the bombers now and knew what was coming their way. The *Ami* air-gangsters would undoubtedly plaster the whole area in their usual indiscriminate manner. What did it matter if they killed a few hundred frog-eaters in the process?

'Yessir,' Dietrich flung a hasty glance at his clipboard. 'Six Tigers, a dozen Skoda self-propelled guns, plus the usual complement of armoured half-tracks.'

* A French paramilitary police unit, formed by the collaborationist Vichy French government, to aid the Germans in their fight against the *Resistance*
** See *Guns at Cassino* for further details

'Excellent –' The word died on Wiese's lips as the first bomb exploded close by like the crack of doom, and the whole bunker swayed and trembled as if struck by a sudden tornado. Plaster came tumbling down in a grey drizzle and for a moment the lights flickered, went out and came on again, as the teleprinters stopped clattering, indicating that the main power supply had been cut. 'All right, Dietrich!' Wiese cried hurriedly above the shouts and curses and the frightened cries of the 'grey mice'.* 'Signal whoever is the commander of SS Assault Regiment Wotan to report to me *immediately*. I don't know how you're going to do it, but even if it means carrying the signal personally by hand, *do it*!' He raised his voice even more as the second stick of bombs came whistling down shrilly. 'And, *meine Herren*, I think it is about time that the headquarters of the 19th Army beat a hasty retreat – I mean, made a strategic withdrawal to a safer place. Come on, *los*!'

He grabbed his cap and next moment was running up the stairs to the surface, followed by a suddenly panicked mob of men and women, fighting and clawing at each other in their haste to escape what would soon be a death-trap.

The long retreat of the German 19th Army had commenced . . .

* Nickname given to the female auxiliaries of the German Army, on account of their grey uniform and mouselike temperament

BOOK ONE

A March to Battle

CHAPTER 1

'*Great crap on the Christmas Tree*!' Sergeant-Major Schulze of SS Assault Regiment Wotan cried in sheer amazement and pushed his cap to the back of his big, shaven skull. 'Willya cast ya frigging glassy orbits at that!'

Next to him in the turret of the lead Tiger, Corporal Matz kicked the driver below with his wooden leg, indicating that the latter should pull up.

Obediently the sweating, grease-streaked youngster did so and the huge sixty-ton monster rolled to a stop. Behind them in the number two Tiger, Colonel von Dodenburg, commander of SS Wotan, signalled to his driver to do the same. Slowly the whole column jammed beneath the cover of the trees fringing both sides of the narrow French country road came to a stop, the panzer grenadiers routinely springing from their half-tracks to take up covering positions in the ditches to each side.

For a moment there was an awed silence, broken only by the steady throb of the motors and the lazy buzzing of the bees among the yellow flowers in the ditches. Before them on their left, just off the road, there was a typical *Wehrmacht* supply depot: a field surrounded by heavy wooden fences of barbed wire, containing tidy mounds of supplies, each one neatly labelled with details of its contents. To the rear there were three wooden huts and a small office over which flew proudly the swastika flag of the Third Reich.

Schulze swallowed hard, his prominent adam's apple going up and down his skinny throat as if carried by an express lift. 'Do you see what I see, apeturd?' he asked, a note of awe, perhaps even reverence, in his voice. 'Cognac . . . champagne . . . *beer*!' He said the word as if it was very holy. '*B - E - E - R*!'

Matz, his leather-faced, wrinkled running-mate, gave a

choking sound, head twisted to one side, as if he were being strangled. 'Don't you dare even to say that word, arse-with-ears!' he croaked. 'In this frigging heat!' He licked cracked, parched lips and felt tenderly his sweat-lathered brow. 'Now look what you've gone and done . . . I think I'm going to get my monthlies.'

'You'll get the toe of my boot up your nasty little keester, if you don't get moving!' von Dodenburg's hard voice cut into their dazed reveries at the sight of so much booze. 'Get over to that sentry next to the gate, Schulze, and find out what we can load up from here. And don't concentrate on the sauce exclusively, either. We need ammunition too,' the tall lean colonel with the bitter mouth of a disappointed man added in warning.

Schulze didn't need a second invitation. He dropped from the turret and in spite of the oppressive heat of this blazing August day doubled to where the ancient sentry in faded field-grey stood staring at them in awe, as if they were a vision from another world. For his part, von Dodenburg took his glasses and began searching the dazzling blue sky carefully. Ever since the new enemy attack in the south and the beginning of their march southwards from Grenoble, the skies had swarmed with enemy tank-busting *Jabos**. It did not pay to be caught out in the open this August. Behind him in the column of half-tracks, the machine-gunners standing up in the open cabs made the same careful scrutiny, swinging their twin guns round warily as they did so.

Ever since they had begun this surprise road march to the south, von Dodenburg had caught his young recruits staring a little apprehensively at the long columns fleeing past them northwards and then gazing at him, as if asking, 'Why in three devils' name are we going south when everyone else is bugging out?' It was a question that von Dodenburg asked himself, too. But the order had come from 19th Army Headquarters itself and von Dodenburg had long given up

* German name for 'dive-bombers'

wondering what went on in the heads of high-ranking staff officers. He supposed, he told himself as he searched the glittering sky metre by metre, he had become a little war-weary and apathetic. Yet, he knew, too, that the fate of those teenage panzer grenadiers, greenbeaks the lot of them, rested squarely on his shoulders. They were all strong, well-behaved farmboys from the mountain farms of the Tyrol, volunteers for the SS to a man. But not one of them had had more than a couple of months of elementary military training. If they ran into trained infantry, they would be slaughtered, unless he and his handful of old hares from the old Wotan protected them. He frowned at the thought. It was a damned heavy responsibility in this summer of 1944 with the Third Reich visibly falling apart.

'Sir . . . sir . . !' It was Schulze.

He let the glasses drop to his chest and stared down at the big red-faced NCO. 'Well?'

'That old prick tells *me*, a senior NCO in the Armed SS' – Schulze poked a thumb like a hairy pork sausage at his chest indignantly – 'that he's not going to allow me in the frigging place without a frigging indent!'

Despite his worries, von Dodenburg's harshly handsome face creased into a smile. Schulze's mind was set on beer, and beer he was going to have. They were all going to have some. 'Corporal Matz!' he barked.

'Sir!' the little one-legged Corporal snapped to attention with an audible click of his wooden leg.

'Get your crooked arse into the driver's seat of Number One and start up.' He grinned wolfishly. 'I'm just going to put an indent into the quartermaster's department. Now move it!'

'*Move it* I will, sir!' Matz cried uproariously, his greedy little eyes almost disappearing into the sea of wrinkles of his face. Next moment he had swung himself into the cab and the thunder of the Tiger's motors broke the heavy oppressive silence of the August afternoon.

Von Dodenburg cupped his hands around his mouth,

while all around the handful of veteran tankers grinned, already knowing what kind of 'indent' the Old Man was going to put in, and cried: 'All right, let's put in our requisition, Corporal Matz. *Ram the frigging gates*!'

'*Yessir*!' Matz chortled with delight and let out the clutch. The sixty-ton monster surged forward and an ecstastic Schulze yelled, 'Go to it, you perverted banana-sucker! *This day I'm gonna dip my dong in suds, I swear it by all that is holy . .* !' As if to emphasize his words, he ripped open the front of his trousers and, whipping out his celebrated organ, waved it like a deadly weapon at the suddenly ashen-faced sentry . . .

Routinely they were cracking the heads off bottles of French *Mutzig Pils* and taking mighty swallows, spitting out the broken glass in the process, as they doubled back and forth loading supplies on the decks of the half-tracks and tanks. Directing operations, Schulze was stripped to the waist, his brawny torso gleaming with sweat, routinely drinking out of his helmet, filled to the brim with fizzy French beer.

For his part, von Dodenburg, happy that his men were happy, strolled around the little camp in a leisurely way, followed by Matz, whose pockets were bulging with bottles of beer, looking for the kind of supplies he knew were going to be in short supply in the days to come. He had soon discovered that there was no fuel worth speaking of, except for a couple of hundred jerricans of petrol, which were already strapped to the sides of the half-tracks as a reserve. However, there was plenty of tinned *Kommissbrot**, great lengths of salami and smoked hams, which would keep for months.

But there were other surprising items in this great food store, which told him just how well the Army of Occupation had lived in these last years in France. Crates of best quality champagne, caviare, goose-liver *pâté*, bottles of truffles, asparagus tips, even huge cartons of contraceptives, as if all

* Army bread

the Army of Occupation had ever done had been to stuff their guts with the delicacies of France and vend their loins on willing French whores.

'Now I can see why they say "to live like God in France",' Matz had commented sourly, picking up a huge jar of olives stuffed with red peppers. 'These frigging rear echelon swine really did live up to the old proverb, while we was getting our asses shot off us in Russia.' Angrily he let the jar drop. It shattered and olives rolled everywhere. Almost routinely Matz picked up another one and was about to do the same, when a deep bass voice commanded: 'I advise you, Corporal, not to do that again. It is a court-martial offence to destroy the property of the *Wehrmacht* without written permission!'

Matz and von Dodenburg swung round, a little startled. A big, heavy-set man had appeared from behind the shed and was standing there, his uniform immaculate, his riding boots gleaming like mirrors. In spite of the oppressive heat, he wore gloves. He saw von Dodenburg's badges of rank, the tarnished stars of an SS colonel on his dirty ragged tunic, and came to the position of attention. Almost contemptuously he raised the riding crop which he affected to the gleaming peak of his cap and rasped: 'Captain Quartermaster Dietz, Commander 18th Corps Supply Depot.'

Carelessly von Dodenburg returned the salute and looked the man up and down, not hiding his disgust with what he saw. The man was a typical *Etappenschwein.* His chest bore not a single decoration, save the War Service Cross, Third Class. Probably all this long bitter war, he had served behind the lines like this, getting fat and rich, without ever having heard a single shot fired in anger.

'*Obersturmbannführer*,' the big fat quartermaster snapped. 'Could I have an explanation for what is taking place here? Surely even an SS officer should know that one cannot take military property from a corps' supply depot without specific written permission from the corps commander himself? Please, may I have an explanation for this outrageous conduct?' His face flushed an even deeper red and his jowls wobbled mightily.

Von Dodenburg's mouth dropped open and he stared at the quartermaster incredulously, unable to speak for a moment. 'Specific written orders!' he gasped finally. 'My God, man, do you live in cloud-cuckoo-land? Don't you know the Army is in full retreat? The world's falling apart and you want a *specific written order*!' He gasped for breath.

The quartermaster was unmoved. He tapped the pile of olive jars with his riding crop and said coldly. 'It says here that there were one hundred jars of olives, quality A, stuffed with assorted peppers. Now there are ninety-nine jars only and I have to account for that missing jar to the quartermaster general at Corps. That is a very grave responsibility.'

Von Dodenburg swallowed. 'God Almighty,' he choked, 'I didn't think that people like you still existed! Don't you know that you've got only a matter of days, perhaps even hours, before the *Amis* and the frog-eaters take over your precious store and do with it just what the devil they like? Christ, man, can't you get it through your damned wooden head? The German Army in southern France is in retreat. *We are beaten*!'

Still the other officer remained unmoved. 'I am a Prussian officer and official and I do my duty as a good Prussian should. Besides, only the other day the Führer proclaimed, "*Die Front steht*!"* and I believe implicitly in our beloved Führer, even if his *own* SS seemingly do not.' His fat face contorted savagely with contempt. 'I have no time for rumour-mongers, cowards and defeatists. I know –' He stopped abruptly and thrust his stomach forward suddenly, as if someone had just given him a great punch in the small of his back. Slowly, very slowly, his fat lips opened and his yellowing false teeth started to bulge through them stupidly, the cheap plastic already flushing with bright red blood. While von Dodenburg and Matz watched in complete bewilderment, mouths gaping open like village yokels, he

* Roughly: 'The front still stands!'

sank to his knees, head bent, and for the first time the two of them could see the ragged scarlet hole that had suddenly appeared in the small of his back. For a long moment the quartermaster knelt there like a boxer fighting off defeat, not wanting to go down for a count of ten. 'Specific . . . written . . .' he gasped in a husky whisper and then with startling suddenness his fat face slammed to the tarmac and he lay there dead among his precious 'olives, quality A, stuffed with assorted peppers', while somewhere to their right the first lazy chatter of an antiquated French machine-gun told a still bemused von Dodenburg that they were under attack . . .

CHAPTER 2

'*The frog-eaters are up there, sir*!' Schulze reported hastily, the beer streaming down his flushed face where he had jammed on his helmet as soon as the firing had commenced. 'Ten o'clock and three o'clock, left and right of the road!' He ducked hastily as a vicious salvo of slugs ripped the length of the pile of cognac bottles behind which they were sheltering, sending glass flying and filling the air abruptly with the stench of brandy.

'Christ on a crutch!' Matz whined in protest. 'Now that's not fair. In fact, it's frigging inhuman, shooting up a poor soldier's sauce like that. It ain't –'

'*Schnauze*!' Schulze cried and obediently Matz closed his 'trap' as the NCO and the officer studied the situation. The two hillsides, studded with thick stunted pines, dominated the little white country road. Even if there were only a few of the damned partisans up there, they could make life highly dangerous for anyone trying to drive up that road.

Schulze seemed to be able to read the tall CO's thoughts, for he said: 'We could button up the Tigers and take them?'

'Perhaps, but they might have bazookas and we'd be sitting ducks packed in that tight pass. Besides, what about the panzer grenadiers in the open half-tracks? Those gunners would slaughter them like cattle.'

Schulze nodded his agreement, while von Dodenburg focused his binoculars, shielding the lenses with one hand so that their glitter would not give his position away to snipers. Now he could see the puffs of white smoke coming from the hillside quite clearly, and here and there a darker figure outlined against the glaring white of the chalk as a *maquis* darted from one position to another. 'One . . . two . . . four . . . machine-guns,' he announced, counting them off, 'with perhaps a score or more of men.'

'*Kleine Fische*!' Matz sneered contemptuously, putting down the bottle of cognac carefully. 'Little fish. Could take 'em all on me lonesome, with one arm tied behind me back. Wotan scared of *that*!' He spat on the ground scornfully.

'This isn't the old Wotan,' von Dodenburg said, trying to make up his mind how to attack. 'The old Wotan died in Italy.'

'Yer,' Schulze agreed, not taking his eyes off their front, 'this shower of shit we're landed with now is a real lot of cardboard soldiers.'

'All right.' Von Dodenburg made his decision. 'Schulze, I want you to pick out a dozen of the old hares and take them up those rocks at ten o'clock. Stick close to the ground and with a bit of luck you'll be on their flank before they know it. In the meantime we'll try to keep their heads down with smoke and HE* from one of the self-propelled guns.' He frowned and looked hard at the big NCO. 'And don't take any foolish risks. I can't afford to lose you, you big rogue.'

'And don't speak to no strange men, either,' Matz added, but the look in his eyes was one of concern. He knew just how dangerous the mission given to his old running-mate was. If he was caught out in the open by one of those frog-eaters' machine-guns . . . Matz shook his head and did not think that particularly unpleasant thought to an end.

Now things happened fast. Von Dodenburg took charge of the Skoda, a captured Russian cannon built on to the chassis of a Skoda-built tank, to form a crude but effective piece of self-propelled artillery. Crouching low beneath the protective shield, directing its progress by means of the periscope, listening to the howl of the slugs richocheting off its armour and the furious patter of machine-gun fire like heavy tropical rain on a tin roof, he found a position where he could bring some fire to bear on the twin hills. He knew he could do little harm to the defenders but at least the high explosive shells, which now began to strike the woods, might frighten the

* High explosive

French into ducking while Schulze outflanked them.

Now he let the sweating gunners get on with it, all of them stripped to the waist, while he swung the periscope round to focus it on Schulze's party.

Veterans that they were, they were moving fast, almost effortlessly, across the face of the hill, darting from cover to cover in twos and threes while the others protected them. Von Dodenburg could make out Schulze quite clearly, nothing could conceal his enormous bulk, as the NCO lumbered forward, balancing an MG 42 on his shoulder as if it were a child's toy. Once von Dodenburg saw him fling himself down and throw the machine-gun to the ground urgently as if he were about to open fire. Von Dodenburg caught his breath. *They had been spotted on the naked rock*! But it proved to be a false alarm and a moment afterwards he was up on his feet again, lumbering forward, crimson-faced and panting, like an enraged bull. One minute later they had all disappeared into the edge of the wood where the French were concealed and von Dodenburg knew he could do no more. 'All right,' he cried, lowering his glasses, 'fire two rounds of smoke, either side of the road.'

He waited for the soft plop of the smoke dischargers on the sides of the half-track. Lazily the smoke bombs curled into the air, heading for their target, and then, not wanting the risk of being surprised by some resistance man armed with a bazooka, he yelled, 'Driver - reverse. At the double now! *Dalli . . . dalli*!'

Hurriedly the sweating driver, half naked like the rest, threw the Skoda into reverse gear and as the bombs exploded to their front, thick white smoke streaming and billowing upwards almost immediately, they scuttled to the rear like a frightened metal beetle. There was nothing more they could do. Now it was up to Schulze . . .

'Great buckets of flying piss!' Matz exclaimed angrily. 'What the frigging hell is he up to, sir?' The little man slammed his clenched fist into the earth where he crouched next to an equally worried von Dodenburg.

The tall officer sucked his teeth. The rattle of machine-guns up the road had ceased dramatically five minutes ago. There had been a series of cries, angry shouts in both German and French, a few single shots, a swift burst of machine-gun fire, a piteous howl of pain, then silence, absolute silence. Since then, *nothing*! No Schulze, grinning all over his big mug, exhibiting some trophy or other, not even a runner to tell them what had happened up there in the twin hills. *Where in three devils' name was the damned NCO*?

'Yer don't think he's bought the farm, sir, do you?' Matz asked anxiously. 'I mean, everybody's luck runs out one day. Heaven, arse and cloudburst, where the fuck is the big bastard?' Again Matz slammed his fist into the baked earth in exasperation. Von Dodenburg flung a glance at his watch. He would give Schulze five minutes. If he hadn't made an appearance by then, he'd chance sending up a half-track. One way or another he had to find out what had happened and whether the way ahead was now clear.

The minutes ticked by leadenly. Now the only sound was the soft hum of the bees and the subdued, worried chatter of the teenage panzer grenadiers. Again von Dodenburg flashed a glance at his watch. One minute to go. He opened his mouth to alert Lieutenant Krings, who would command the half-track, and in that very instant there came an unearthly howl from the hills, a scream of absolute, unbearable agony like that of some terrified trapped wild animal, which sent the small hairs flying erect on the back of von Dodenburg's head. Next to him, Matz shivered violently, as if he had just been struck by an icy arctic wind. 'God in heaven,' he quavered, dark eyes wild and wide with fear, '*what was that*?'

Von Dodenburg swallowed hard. He rose to his feet with an effort of naked willpower and unslung his machine-pistol. Now the shrill scream had died away to a low mournful keening, which in its own way was as terrifying as the screaming had been, as if whoever it was had realized that there was no hope for him; that he was condemned to be slaughtered like some dumb animal. 'I don't know, but I intend to find out. Krings, you take over. All right, Matz, grab your weapon. Let's go and earn our pay this day.' Matz nodded wordlessly.

A moment later the two lone figures were moving up the side of that burning white country road towards the hills and the unknown.

'*Sale con*!' the naked man said in a choked voice between gritted teeth. He pursed his lips as if he were about to spit at his torturer. He didn't get the chance. The dark uniformed policeman, with the beret of the *Milice* set jauntily at the side of his head, slammed his cruelly nailed mountain-boot into the prisoner's face. Something snapped and dark-red blood jetted from his nostrils. His spine arched and he screamed hideously.

The officer standing above him laughed and, taking the stub of the cheap black cigar out of his thin lips, he spat contemptuously on the prisoner's tortured genitals. '*Bon . . .*' he rasped in a husky voice, coarsened by years of cheap cigars and even cheaper drink. '*Fini la grande guerre*.' He drew a dirty finger under his throat to make his meaning quite clear.

The *Milice* clicked back the bolt of his Mauser, while the naked prisoner stared up at him petrified with terror, meaningless sounds coming from his cracked and thickened lips. The policeman took aim casually. The watchers could see how his right shoulder muscles hardened and how the finger gripping the trigger grew white as he took first pressure. There was absolute, total silence. The shot rang out with startling suddenness. Even the other police jumped.

The prisoner's head seemed to fly apart. Suddenly the back of his skull was a sickening red, oozing mass, through which the shattered bone gleamed brightly like polished ivory.

Calmly the killer ejected the spent cartridge and it fell to the white dust, now steadily turning a dull crimson with the escaping blood.

The officer nodded his approval and, rolling his cigar to the side of his mouth, he said to the man crouched over the little fire of twigs and branches they had snapped from the pines, '*Allez, vite avec le feu* . . .'

'*Oui, mon commandant*,' the policeman said and started blowing hard to start up the flames.

Von Dodenburg burst through the last of the trees and stopped short at the scene before him. The dead *maquis* sprawled on the barren rock in the extravagant pose of one done to death violently; the hard faced *Milice* everywhere, some of them busy engaged in looting the dead; his own men standing watching in awestruck silence (even Schulze was keeping his mouth closed); and above all the French major.

Dry, hot-eyed and dark, with clipped grey hair and a moustache that had the carbonised iridescence of coke, he seemed a burnt-out case, as if consumed by some inner fire. Even his voice had a husky rasp, as of cinders. A dangerous man, von Dodenburg told himself, a very dangerous man.

'What is going on –' he began, stepping forward into the open, and stopped short.

The policeman crouching at the fire had turned. In his hand he held a glowing, red-hot iron of the kind von Dodenburg remembered from his boyhood on his father's estate in East Prussia: the kind the tenant farmers had used for branding sheep.

'*C'est fini, mon commandant*,' the policeman reported.

'*Bon*,' the officer said. He tossed away his cigar hurriedly and accepted the glowing iron, dark eyes burning dangerously from those charred eye-sockets. '*Sale petite garce d'espion*!' he rasped. Next moment he bent and applied the iron to the dead man's soft underbelly. There was the stench of burning flesh, an unholy sizzling which sent a cold finger of fear tracing its way down the small of von Dodenburg's back, and the dead man's legs jerked upwards convulsively, as if he could still feel pain. '*Gott in Himmel*!' Matz cried and next instant he turned away and began to retch miserably against the nearest tree.

Von Dodenburg felt the hot vomit flood his throat too, and he clenched his fists hurriedly to prevent himself from being sick. Instead he strode forward, machine-pistol clenched in his hot sticky fists, eyes gleaming dangerously. '*Monsieur*,' he demanded in his awkward French, '*que vous faites? Dites-moi – vite*!' Even as he spoke, he could see what the *Milice* had done to the dead man's genitals. Hastily he took his gaze off that gory scarlet hole.

The French police major turned round, without haste, as if he had been expecting von Dodenburg and rasped in the guttural German of the Alsace, '*Obersturmbannführer von Dodenburg, ja*?'

Caught completely off guard, von Dodenburg came to an awkward stop and stammered, 'Yes, that is correct . . . And who are you, may I ask?'

The French officer raised his hand to his cap in salute in that slow deliberate way of the Legion, to which he had once belonged in another age, and rasped: 'Major Marcel Marchant, *Obersturmbannführer*, commander of the Third Battalion the *Milice*.' He paused, his hand still raised to his beret and his tough, dark face cracked into a grin, but there was no answering warmth in his eyes. 'Around these parts they call me . . . *the Angel of Death*!'

CHAPTER 3

The drunken Germans and the French police ran riot in the looted corps store, while Marchant and von Dodenburg conferred in the office of the dead quartermaster, still lying stiff and unburied in the dust outside. They danced around with great hams speared on their bayonets, knocking the heads off expensive bottles of best French champagne and guzzling it down as if it were water, taking a few puffs at fine Havana cigars before tossing them away to light another one.

In the cookhouse, in the process of attempting to show the SS just how a real French omelette was made, the drunken cops had covered the range with a great bubbling yellow mess which had long ago oozed up and out of the frying pans, while drunken SS carried away by it all were pelting eggs against the walls and allowing the contents to drip, shell and all, into this monstrous 'omelette'.

'Let them, Colonel,' Marchant had said at the beginning of their talk. 'Let them get the piss and vinegar out of their systems. They'll never get another opportunity like this again.' He took a drag at the cheap working-man's cigar that he preferred and said quite simply, as if it were a statement of fact, 'After all, we *are* all doomed men.'

Von Dodenburg stared at him in the cool gloom of the dead quartermaster's office, wondering for a moment if the Frenchman was joking. But he wasn't. His tough, cynical face at that moment revealed a depth of despair that von Dodenburg had never come across before. 'Is the situation that serious?'

Marchant nodded. 'As long as iron can take a point, watch your backs,' he rasped, his dark-eyed gaze boring into von Dodenburg as if he were trying to teach him an important lesson. 'The trees grow cudgels . . . wear your helmet . . . String can strangle, so watch your throat. You see what I am trying to say, Colonel? Every man's hand is now against us. Dark nights are dangerous – *never walk alone*!'

Von Dodenburg tried to defuse the tension. Pitching his voice soft and low, trying not to hear the drunken laughter and raucous noise from outside, he said, 'So you have been sent by General Wiese to escort us across the mountains and that is why you killed that naked man. He had betrayed our approach march to the *maquis*. Yes?'

Marchant dipped the end of his cigar in the glass of cognac in front of him, suddenly thoughtful, even moody, and nodded. 'Yes. Now all those who have lived off the Germans – and lived well off them, I must say – these last four years are trying to get on the liberation bandwagon, currying favour with information and deeds before it is too late. But for me,' he shrugged in that expressive Gallic fashion, 'there is no hope. They will shoot me – at the best. At the worst – well . . .' He didn't complete the thought. Instead he said, 'That is why I brand my initials on the pigs. "MM" – Marcel Marchant, then they'll know who passed this way.' He looked at von Dodenburg with such hot-eyed intensity that the former was forced to lower his gaze.

Outside someone was saying thickly, 'Will none of you piss-pansies get me out of this sodding barrel . . . I'll either have to drink mesen to death or drown in the frigging suds!'

'In Forty when you came,' Marchant said thoughtfully, almost as if talking to himself, moodily puffing at his cigar, 'I had just transferred from Legion to Metropolitan France to take over a company of conscript infantry up the Maginot Line. And do you know what the pricks did when they spotted the first Bo . . . er, German tank? They flung away their weapons and ran off back home to mother – *and they were protected by two metres of solid concrete and steel*! That did it for me. Their fathers back in 1914 had fought for four years, three million of them giving their lives for *la belle France*. But those pricks of mine had been indoctrinated by the lousy communists and socialists, *les sales cons* of the Popular Front *not* to fight.' He flashed von Dodenburg that bitter hot-eyed look of his. 'I swore then on the day of the surrender that I would fight to the death to free France from the red rabble, even if I had to work with you, the Germans, to do so. *Eh bien*,' he shrugged again, 'so I did for four long years, and by God, I am going to go down fighting. I'll either beat the Red rabble or they'll kill me!'

Von Dodenburg was shocked by such naked vehemence and fanaticism. He had not heard people talk like that since the days of 1940, the year of victory, when the messes of the Armed SS had been filled with tough young men eager to die for their Führer and the vaunted New Order in Europe. Now they were all long dead, buried in some forgotten Russian steppe. '*Commandant* Marchant, let us get down to business. What is to be our route of march? I want to avoid all action with the resistance, if possible. I must keep up the strength of my effectives in order to carry out whatever task General Wiese assigns me. You understand that?'

'Yes, I understand *Obersturmbannführer*. A good commander never throws away the lives of his men needlessly.' He took a drag at his cigar. 'We do the unexpected, *Obersturmbannführer*,' he said after a moment.

'*Unexpected*?'

'Yes. We go through the Vercors *Massif*. It is shaped like a gigantic arrowhead some sixty kilometres long by thirty wide. It has always been a citadel and in these last years when the Red rabble and their turncoats started to come out of their damned holes,' he spat on the floor in disgust, 'they used it as their last-ditch defensive position.' Marchant saw the suddenly worried look on the German officer's face and said hurriedly, 'Please don't misunderstand me. I am not challenging them for the sake of the challenge.' He grinned softly. 'The Angel of Death has no wish to die – just yet. No, my guess is that they won't think we will challenge them in the heart of their own stronghold. They will think we will attempt to use the roads around the Vercors *Massif* and will concentrate their forces, knowing that the few roads there are till we reach the plain of the Rhône can be easily ambushed.'

Slowly von Dodenburg nodded his head in approval. It was a tactic after his own heart. Catch the enemy off balance, strike where your opponent least expects. 'But what about my Tigers? They are very heavy,' he said thoughtfully, still mulling the idea over in his head. 'Do you think they can make it?'

'Come, I will show you.' Marchant rose to his feet hurriedly, and automatically slung the soldier's rifle he always carried over his shoulder.

Von Dodenburg smiled slightly. Fanatic he might be, but by carrying the rifle he was making sure that no sniper would identify him as an officer and pick him off first. Together they pushed their way through the confused mass of drunken cops and SS, watched over by the terrified old men who had originally guarded the depot, now staring helplessly at the scenes all around them, as if the world had gone crazy; which in a way it had.

The two of them paused outside the noisy camp, standing in the shade cast on the brilliant white road by the green elms. 'There,' Marchant said, pointing to the west, 'that is the Vercors *Massif*. Something, eh?'

Slowly von Dodenburg nodded his agreement. 'Something indeed,' he said softly, staring at the immense gaunt rampart of rock, which barred their way to the Rhône plain. It seemed a landscape designed for drama, a stark natural acropolis, the soaring white limestone cliffs furrowed with caves gouged into them by the wind and rain, a few scraggy trees dotting it here and there with dark green. 'Does anyone else live up there - save your Red rabble?'

Marchant shook his head. 'When we go in there, *Obersturmbannführer*,' he answered sombrely, 'the only people we will meet will be the enemy. From now onwards it will be *shoot first and ask questions afterwards*!'

'And when do we march?'

Marchant didn't answer von Dodenburg's question directly. Instead he pointed to the right of the road beyond the twin hills now occupied by one of his companies, unfortunates who

THE SITUATION IN SOUTHERN FRANCE, AUGUST 1944

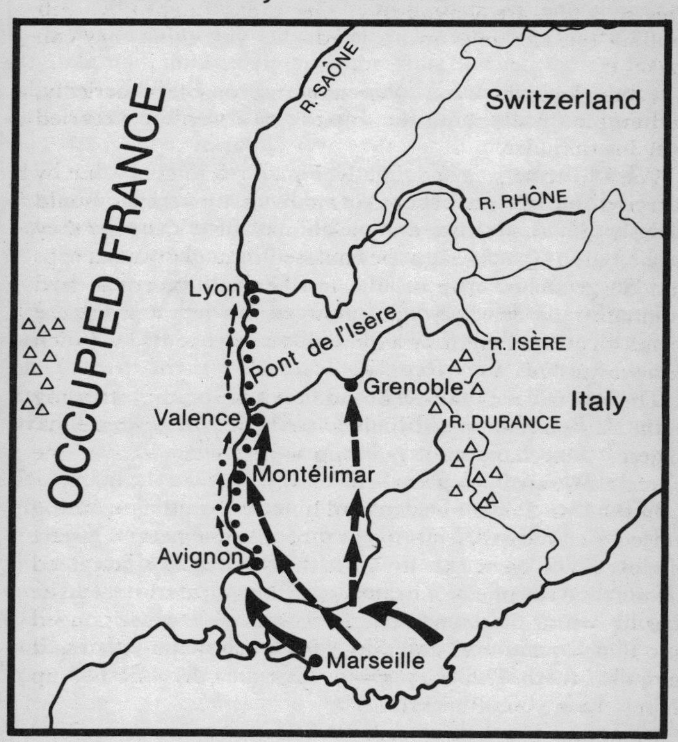

Legend

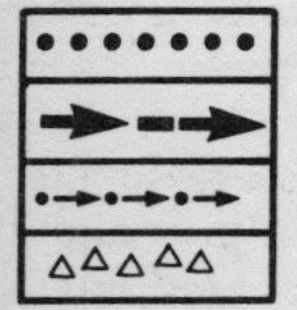

Route Nationale Seven

US Seventh Army Advance Route

French First Army Advance Route

Mountains

had not been let loose to enjoy the delights of the German supply depot. 'Do you see the flash?'

Hastily von Dodenburg flung up his glasses. 'Yes, I can see it. Someone is watching us.'

'Exactly. Whoever it is will report our move to the Red rabble and they will start immediately making their plans to ambush us.' He puffed at his cigar and von Dodenburg could almost feel Marchant's mind racing, as he worked out what to do next. 'So we must use the cover of darkness to fool them.'

'Fool them?'

'Yes, make them believe we are living up to the reputation of the *Milice* and the Armed SS – ruthless drunken mobs, lacking any kind of discipline, once they take to drink.'

He grinned abruptly and von Dodenburg grinned with him. 'So that is why you encouraged the men to get drunk?'

'Of course. And they will continue to carouse far into the night, just as that Red rabble expects them to do. The watchers will see that from their fires and the racket they kick up . . . But of course,' he added softly, 'by then we will have long before vanished into the *Massif*.'

'But who will keep the fires going . . . make the noise, kick up the racket?' von Dodenburg objected, a little puzzled. By way of an answer, Marchant pointed to the nearest guard, a white-haired ancient in faded, wrinkled field-grey, who leaned on his rifle as if he needed all the support it could give to his weary old bones.

Von Dodenburg looked at the French major aghast. 'But you know what will happen to them once the *maquis* find out they have been tricked. They'll massacre the poor old bastards without mercy.'

Marchant shrugged elegantly. 'Let us get this straight right from the outset, *Obersturmbannführer* von Dodenburg.' His dark eyes flashed fire as he stared hard at the German. 'That is outlaw country up there, no quarter given or expected. We'll even have to be cruel to our own kind, if we are to survive. Our mission, the saving of a whole army, is more important than the lives of a handful of impotent old men, who will die soon anyway.' He gasped for breath and von Dodenburg could see how he was being consumed by the inner fire once more. 'From now onwards it is, as we used to say in the old days in the Legion, *marchez ou crevez*! That means in German –'

'I know what it means,' von Dodenburg interrupted that hectic flow of impassioned words sombrely and stared at that vast monolithic cathedral of rock to their front which dominated the plain of the Rhône, through which now they must fight their way. 'It means – march or die . . .'

All passion had vanished from Marchant's voice when he spoke again, as if suddenly he too had realized the full meaning of that brutal old phrase. The ash from his cigar fell to the dust, as if his hand had abruptly trembled. 'March or die,' he echoed in a hoarse whisper and then, without another word, turned and began to walk back into the camp, shoulders bowed, as if bearing an almost intolerable load. For a moment more von Dodenburg remained standing there, staring at that gaunt mountain range, the dark shadows of the approaching night already beginning to sweep across its peak like some great silent bird, and then he too turned and followed . . .

CHAPTER 4

It was a beautiful cloudless day. Already it was warm in the mountains although it was still early morning, and the heat rippled in a blue haze over the peaks which dominated the valley floor below. Like an enormous metal centipede the long column of armour and trucks crawled in first gear along the road which wound in and out of the valley, following the concave, curving shape of the mountain wall to the right.

Up front Schulze, sober again now, but with a raging thirst and bloodshot eyes, commanded the lead Tiger, with von Dodenburg following in a half-track laden with panzer grenadiers. Behind, spaced at fifty-metre intervals, came the rest of the tanks and half-tracks. Behind them came Marchant's *Milice* in their trucks bringing up the rear. In case of trouble, Schulze's Tiger was to button up the road, while the panzer grenadiers swung off the track and doubled into the shallow stream to their left. They would deal with any opposition, while Marchant's *Milice* similarly sealed off the rear. As von Dodenburg, the veteran of partisan warfare on the Russian front, had snapped to a pensive Marchant before the convoy had set off into the mountains, 'The whole trick, Major, is not to allow yourself to be cut into little groups – the old salami tactic.'

'Yes, I know,' Marchant had agreed. 'It is the same tactic that that Red rabble employs if it can.' He gave von Dodenburg that burning sardonic smile of his and said, 'United we stand, divided we fall, eh?'

Von Dodenburg had not returned the smile. Instead he had snapped severely, knowing he had to reassert his authority as the commander of this operation, 'There will be no talk of *falling*, Marchant, or *failing*. SS Assault Regiment Wotan *never* fails. All right, that's all. Let's move out.'

Marchant had looked suitably impressed . . .

Now they rolled through that awesome landscape, their engines roaring, the rumble and clatter of the tracks echoing and re-echoing in the tight chasm. Standing next to Schulze, the sweat glazing his face as if with grease, Matz took a last sip from his flatman, flung it over the side of the turret and said conversationally, 'Have you ever thought what you're gonna do when this war is over, plush-ears?'

'Plush-ears, yersen!' Schulze snorted, telling himself he would give his right arm for a litre of ice-cold, foaming Bavarian suds. 'This frigging war is never gonna end, so why frigging worry?'

'Course it'll end, the Führer'll snuff it some time and then we'll all be lovey-dovey agen and holding hands, and sweetness and light will reign throughout the world.'

Schulze was not impressed by such noble thoughts. He growled, 'Frigging sweetness and light will reign, my sainted arse! The frigging shit will rain down on us poor old horses' arses, that's what'll *rain*.'

'Ha, ha!' Matz laughed hollowly. 'So you made a frigging joke, ha-frigging-ha!' His brow furrowed in a frown which indicated serious contemplation. 'No, I asked you a serious question and I expect a serious answer, comrade.'

'Don't you frigging *comrade* me, you little crippled piss-pansy! I ain't your comrade, I am a senior non-commissioned officer in the –' He stopped short, his headache, the raging thirst and Matz's question forgotten immediately. 'Hey,' he snapped urgently, 'what do you make of that, Matzi?'

'What?'

'*That*!'

Matz followed the direction of Schulze's outstretched hand and gasped. Nailed to one of the telegraph posts that ran the length of the valley road there was a skeleton, the like of which he remembered from the anatomy room of the local girls' school into which he had sneaked as a randy teenager in the days before the war, when they had been looking for what they called 'dirty books'. But this skeleton was slightly different. It bore a German helmet and there was no mistaking what was represented by the lock of black hair escaping from beneath it and the other piece of hair stuck under the twin holes of the nostrils.

'Holy strawsack,' Matz gasped as, below, the driver instinctively braked to a halt at the strange spectacle, 'it's supposed to be . . . the . . . *the fucking Führer*!'

'*Death to the Germans*!' read the crudely printed sign placed at the feet of the skeleton, probably stolen by the *maquis* from some local school. And the sign, plus the caricature of the Führer, had kept the Wotan troopers occupied for at least ten minutes before von Dodenburg had managed to get the column moving again.

It had been followed half an hour later by a real corpse, that of a woman in the uniform of the *Milice* hanging from one of the telegraph posts and slowly rotating in the faint hot wind, her skirts tied up around her waist to reveal what they had done to her with the pole, the blood still trickling an ugly black down the inside of her pale thighs.

Von Dodenburg had just prevented himself retching at the very last moment and had hurriedly summoned up Marchant from the rear of the column. He had come up in a cloud of dust, weaving in and out of the stalled column in his captured jeep, and had identified her at once. 'Colonel Maude,' he had announced staring up at those savagely ravaged loins sombrely, 'that is what the *maquis* nicknamed her. She was the mistress of the district *Milice* chief. She hated the Red rabble with a passion. *Mon Dieu*, I remember how she once roasted the arse of one of those commie intellectuals in a frying pan at the Hotel Bellier –' he stopped abruptly and said urgently, '*Obersturmbannführer*, you know what they're trying to do, don't you?'

With a nod von Dodenburg indicated that Schulze should take care of the tortured Frenchwoman and said, grateful for not having to look at her any more, 'No.'

'They're trying to hold us up, that's what they are trying to do. First the skeleton, then this, and there'll be more. Perhaps a road-block, some sniping,' he shrugged eloquently, 'anything to make us waste time.'

'But why?' von Dodenburg asked. 'If they are going to attack us, why not get on with it? Piss or get off the pot!' he added savagely, as behind him on the ground a cursing Schulze tried to lever the pole free with dreadful sucking sounds that made the small hairs at the back of his head stand on end.

'Because our night departure from that depot fooled the Red rabble. They probably ambushed the main roads *around* the *Massif*, not expecting us, as I had anticipated, to go *through* it.'

'Oh for God's sake, don't be so self-satisfied and smug,' von Dodenburg burst out, desperate for this conversation to end so that he could get away from this place of horror. Behind him Schulze cursed and cursed as he fought to free the dead woman.

Marchant shrugged in that careless French way. Why was the Boche taking on so about a tortured piece of gash? Both sides, Vichy and the Resistance, had been doing this sort of thing for years now in the bitter secret war which had been waged throughout occupied France. Nobody could hurt a Frenchman like another Frenchman. '*Eh bien*, the Reds haven't much in the way of transport so they are making their way over the mountains on cycles, carts, anything with wheels, hurrying to cut us off here before we descend to the plain of the Rhône. So they try to hold us up with their tricks.'

But for once Commandant Marcel Marchant, the Angel of Death, was wrong. On this brilliant August day in 1944, the Western Allies were putting into operation the first of their bold schemes to prevent General Wiese's 19th Army escaping to the north to join up with their hard-pressed comrades. Already, as with a sigh of relief Schulze freed the pole and at last managed to pull the dead woman's skirts down to hide that dreadful sight, the attackers were on their way . . .

*

Most of that long hot afternoon passed in weary silence, save for those strange far-off howls in the surrounding hills which reminded those of the old hares who had served on the Eastern Front of the cries of the half-starved steppe wolves they had seen gnawing at the frozen bodies of their dead comrades in the snow. '*Himmel, Arsch und Wolkenbruch*!' Schulze, unnerved by the business of the murdered woman, cursed more than once. 'What the devil have the frogs got howling up there?'

His only answer, each time, was the dismal howl from above, which set his heart off beating electrically like a trip-hammer. It was just after four, when von Dodenburg ordered a short rest in order that the men might eat and drink and carry out essential maintenance on the tracked vehicles, the tracks of which had become loose due to the constant turning of bends in the mountain road, that the strange howling was forgotten. For it had been replaced by a solemn droning from the south, which became louder and louder by the minute. All eyes turned in that direction, the men standing around the vehicles, heads drenched and dripping with water from the stream, peering against the sun, trying to make out what it might be.

And then there they were! Two huge Vs of four-engined bombers plodding purposefully through the brilliant afternoon sky, stretched out over kilometres, each bomber towing behind it two large silent gliders.

Matz whistled softly through the gap in his front teeth and next to him Schulze said solemnly, as he shaded his eyes against the glare of the sun, 'Now the clock is well and truly in the pisspot!'

It certainly was.

Von Dodenburg realized immediately what was happening. In the summer of 1944 the once proud German *Luftwaffe* did not have capability of launching an airborne invasion of such dimensions – there had to be at least a couple of hundred planes and gliders heading their way. Those planes were Allied and they were coming in to drop their paras and gliderborne troops right on the road that led from the south up to Lyon along the Rhône valley. Marchant had been wrong. The 'Red rabble', as he always called them, had tried to hold up Wotan so that they would not reach the plain in time to stop the enemy paras cutting off the German 19th Army. *They had been tricked*!

Now all was controlled excitement and frenzied haste, as the *Milice* and the panzer grenadiers prepared for the great dash to the Rhône valley. Men ran back and forth, unloading unessential equipment to lighten the loads of the trucks and half-tracks. Red-faced NCOs bellowed angry orders. Officers shrilled their whistles and consulted their maps by means of the little blue torches clipped to their tunics. Drivers checked their engines and filled up their tanks from the jerricans. Everywhere the tension mounted as the mixed force of Frenchmen and Germans prepared for the battle to come, the muted sound of cannonfire and the sharp angry snap-and-crackle of small-arms fire already being wafted across the mountains from where the enemy paras had begun the battle with the 19th Army.

Von Dodenburg and Marchant were here, there and everywhere, urging their men to ever greater efforts; making them eat and drink on the double; clearing the greenbeaks out of the ditches where they seemed to be urinating all the time, their nerves on edge at the prospect of their first battle; checking and re-checking that every gun was loaded, that the machine-gunners in the half-tracks had equal supplies of HE and AP* ammunition – a hundred and one tasks to be carried out on the run, while to the west the battle between the paras and the 19th Army developed ominously.

It was only five minutes before the excited, nervous column

* Armour-piercing

was ready to move out that von Dodenburg had time to break the bad news to Schulze, in charge of the Tigers and the Skodas: 'You know the problem, don't you, you big rogue?' he asked without preliminaries.

'Yessir,' Schulze replied promptly. 'We're just too damned big and slow.' He took a nervous puff at his cigarette, his big, broad honest face abruptly worried in the red glow.

'Exactly. Speed is of the essence and the armour will slow us up, though we will need it urgently down in the plain once we engage the *Amis*.'

'So you want us to go it alone, sir?' Schulze said deliberately. He took another puff at his cigarette and threw it away with a sudden angry gesture. 'Dicey,' he added.

'*I know it's shitting dicey*!' von Dodenburg exploded angrily, the tension beginning to tell. 'But there is nothing I can do about it. It's not a perfect world, damn it!'

'Sorry, sir,' Schulze was immediately conciliatory. He knew the strain the CO was under. 'Don't worry, sir. Weeds never die,' he forced himself to say in his normal cheerful, booming tone.

On the turret above him in the gloom, Matz, who knew exactly the risks armour ran at night, moving without the support of infantry to ward off enemy missilemen, moaned and said solemnly, 'Famous frigging last words . . . famous frigging last words indeed . . .'

Five minutes later the last of the trucks had disappeared into the velvet gloom, heading for the sound of the battle, leaving them there, suddenly aware that the hounds – or whatever they were – were beginning to howl again . . .

CHAPTER 5

The glider came hurtling out of the night. A sudden hiss. A vague swishing. And there it was – a great black shadow sweeping across the pale orbs of their upturned faces. Next moment it slammed into the ground. A great cloud of dust. Its brakes howled as the pilot tried desperately to stop its crazy ride across the open field. The barbed wire tied around its sleds to assist the braking snapped like twine. Now there was an ear-splitting howl. Canvas and wood ripped and tore. By some miracle, the pilot missed a clump of oaks. A wing snapped. It fell off like a severed limb. The glider lurched crazily, slithered round in a wild circle, throwing up a huge wake of dust, and came to an abrupt stop.

Von Dodenburg didn't hesitate. As the first of the bemused glidermen came to and slammed the door open with a thrust of his shoulder, he cried at the top of his voice: '*FIRE*!'

His men, hidden in the ditches all around the field, needed no urging. They opened up with all they had. What happened next was not war; it was murder – the sheer, pitiless massacre of the defenceless Americans. Instead of being greeted by the shouts of welcome, the bottles of wine, the handshakes of the *Resistance*, they were met by a hail of fire.

Uncomprehending, stunned, confused by this terrible thing that was happening to them, they spun round and collapsed, a mess of flailing arms and legs, like puppets in the hands of a puppet-master suddenly gone crazy.

Most of them lay where they fell. Others tried frantically to fight their way out of the bloody mess of dead and dying men jamming the door. The Wotan troopers didn't give them a chance. They poured volley after volley into them. Screaming and shrieking at the tops of their voices, legs and arms jerking as they were hit over and over again at such short range, they dropped on the grotesquely stacked bodies of their slaughtered comrades.

Von Dodenburg had seen enough. He grabbed a grenade from his boot, pulled out the china pin, and with a grunt heaved it straight at the pile of men jamming the door of the stricken glider. It exploded with a throaty crump. Bodies sailed through the air. He caught one horrifying glimpse of a severed head rolling away like an abandoned football. The next instant the ammunition the glider contained exploded. It heaved like a live thing and in a flash it was burning fiercely and the Wotan troopers were turning their attention to the next glider coming soaring in – right into the trap . . .

Half a kilometre away Major Marchant and his *Milice* were para-hunting. On all sides the flares were sailing down, colouring the fields and woods an unearthly flickering green hue, as the Americans came floating down. '*Like pheasant on the wing*,' Marchant chortled, snapping off shot after shot at the descending paras. 'Come, my brave Americans, come and be killed . . . *Welcome to France*!' He laughed crazily at his own macabre humour and, taking deliberate aim, shot at a big burly figure sailing down to his right. The American howled in sheer animal agony as the bullet exploded in his belly, ripping it apart, so that his intestines, steaming furiously in the cold night air, slipped out obscenely. Marchant yelled with delight.

A shot slammed into the tree next to him, showering him with wood splinters. The grin vanished from his brutal face. He swung round. Hanging from a tree twenty metres away an American was trapped by his parachute, the shrouds hopelessly entangled in its branches. In the flickering eerie light he could see the boyish face underneath the big helmet, set in a mixture of fear and defiance. He raised his rifle slowly.

The boy was quicker. He pressed the trigger of his machine-pistol. It erupted into angry life. A stream of white and red tracer zipped lethally towards Marchant. He ducked hastily, severed leaves and branches showering down all around him like green rain.

For a moment he just crouched there. He knew he was safe. The trapped American had used up a whole magazine in that furious burst. He lit one of his cheap cigars, then stepped boldly into the clearing, his rifle raised. 'Stop that!' he barked threateningly, jerking up his rifle.

The boy froze and the magazine he had been trying to fit into his weapon dropped from his nerveless fingers to the ground. 'But . . . but you are French!' he stuttered in tolerable French. 'Why are shoo . . . shooting at me . . . *Nous sommes des parachutistes faisant partie de débarquement allie . . .*' There was a note of absolute, total disbelief in his young voice. Marchant took his time. He was enjoying this confrontation with the first American he had ever met. '*Allies*,' he said slowly, savouring the word, as if it was important. Ignoring the murder and mayhem going on all around him as his cops slaughtered the slowly descending paras, he puffed at his cigar, as if he had all the time in the world. Helplessly the young American stared down at him. 'So you think you have come to *liberate* us, eh, American?' He spat out the word as if it was obscene.

'But they told us that back in Italy,' the young man choked, eyes wide and wild with fear, his face hollowed out to a red skull in the reflected glow of the flares still dropping on that field of death. 'We were coming to free you from the Nazis!'

'How do you think we have lived these last four years?' Marchant snorted. 'We have lived well under the boche. The bourgeoisie have got fat, the workers have had jobs in their war industry, and the whores,' he chuckled obscenely, but there was no warmth in the sound, 'have provided themselves with nice fat nest-eggs, servicing the field-greys. Who cared about that fool de Gaulle until you invaded Normandy? French people just wanted to get on with living their lives in peace, just as they had done back in Thirty-Nine. But you came and suddenly we had a *Resistance*,' he sneered. 'A bunch of Reds and turncoats eager to save their precious skins be-

cause they had grown fat on the boche. *Liberation, I shit on it!*'
Suddenly the thread snapped. He could stand the sight of the young fool with his innocent, well-fed American face no longer. He raised his rifle.
'*No!*' the boy shrieked, cowering there, raising his hands in front of his face like some frightened child trying to blot out a nightmare. '*Please . . . N–O!*'
Carried away by that terrible fire and rage that always burned within him, Marchant pressed the trigger. The rifle butt thumped into his shoulder pleasurably. The boy screamed. Next moment his head slumped to one side and he was dead . . .

Now the survivors of that terrible massacre were either surrendering or stumbling back in dazed and frightened little groups over the bodies of their dead comrades, trying to find cover before the SS counter-attacked. Here and there American mortar crews had managed to set up their small two-inch mortars and there was the obscene belch of mortar bombs howling through the night sky.
Von Dodenburg did not seem to notice. He was too concerned with the attack to come. Marchant, bleeding badly from a deep gash over his right eye, was eager, too, to jump off. While his cops fumbled with their bayonets, their faces taut and glazed as if with grease in the ruddy light of the fires, he snapped, 'A decisive attack is what we need, *Obersturmbannführer*. See them off for good before they have time to dig in and whistle up reinforcements by air at dawn.'
Von Dodenburg nodded coolly, as he snapped another magazine into his machine-pistol. 'What we need, Major, is my damned armour. A couple of Tigers and I could run those damned paras back to the sea for good. *Himmelherrje*,' he burst out, not able to restrain his anger and impatience any longer, 'what in God's name is keeping Schulze and the damned armour?' A mortar bomb exploded nearby and in the brilliant flash of cherry-red flame, von Dodenburg stared

angrily at the *Massif*. But it remained obstinately empty of tanks. There was still no sign of Schulze's Tigers.

Von Dodenburg looked at his wrist-watch. 'All right, Marchant, we attack in five minutes. And you'd better pray that we winkle them out by dawn. Because if we don't,' he looked hard at the Frenchman, 'General Wiese's 19th Army is going to find its route north cut for good . . .'

Schulze stared at the half-moon which darted out of the clouds now and again to illuminate the cold pale face of the rock wall. In spite of the fact that his men were everywhere busy shovelling aside the fall of rock which barred further progress across the valley floor, he felt a strange, eerie sense of loneliness. Involuntarily he shuddered and tightened his grip on the *Schmeisser*.

Behind him, Matz bellowed orders at the sweating tankers as they wrenched at the stone-fall, while the guards that Schulze had placed around the stalled column paced back and forth, obviously nervous and tense, staring time and time again at the mountain. 'Wolves,' Schulze heard them say anxiously. 'Do you think there's wolves up there?'

Again there came that thin dismal howl which set the small hairs standing up erect on the back of his big neck, drifting down the rockside, seeming to go on for ever. 'Holy Mother of God,' he whispered hoarsely to himself, 'what in three devils' name is it?' He stared nervously into the silver gloom, heart in his mouth, nerves tingling electrically, fighting hard against the temptation to fire a wild burst into the stunted bushes . . .

And then there it was. A dark shape slinking down the trail towards them, silent, sinister, ominous, filling the clean night air with its nauseating, raunchy smell.

Schulze jerked up his machine-pistol. Behind him Matz exclaimed, 'What the frigging hell is *that*, Schulze?' He gulped. 'A wolf?'

Schulze stared at the creature emerging from the gloom, snout stuck up, long ears erect, moving forward in a queer kind of slither, as if it were skidding along on its belly. Behind it other dark shapes were beginning to appear, too. There must have been a good score of them, all advancing in that strange, eerily silent manner.

'I asked you what it was, plush-ears,' Matz persisted, his voice trembling, as he too spotted the others.

'Ner, they're not wolves,' Schulze grunted between gritted teeth. 'Some kind of wild dog.' He pressed his trigger. A stream of white tracer hissed towards the advancing animals – and missed.

The wild dogs, if that was what they were, did not seem to notice. They continued their soft-footed, slithering advance.

Abruptly the moon came out from behind the clouds to shine with full force. Schulze gasped and felt an icy finger of fear trace its way down the small of his back, as he saw the froth gleaming a frightening silver around the muzzle of the leading wild dog.

In a moment of total recall he remembered that snowy day back in Russia when they had brought the injured man into the peasant *isba.** The terrible disease he had contracted had already begun to rage. Suddenly he had flung himself free from his helpers and backed against the great green oven that almost filled the hut, eyes bulging from his head, face glazed with sweat, teeth bared like those of some trapped wild animal, the froth bubbling at the corners of his mouth. 'Give the poor sod some water!' one of the helpers had cried. '*Los*, he needs a drink badly!'

Then the full horror had started. Someone had thrust a canteen of water at the injured man and he had reeled back against the stove, eyes wild and horror-stricken, as if the helper had been about to brand him, strange, meaningless, animal-like sounds coming from deep down within him. 'But he don't want to drink,' they had said, voices filled with awe. 'Why?'

The MO had told them a few minutes afterwards. 'There is

* Hut

no hope for him. Look at the bite on his leg.' He had pointed to the ragged, inflamed bite on the man's leg, clearly visible through the torn trousers.

'But we've got to help the poor shit,' someone had objected. 'Can't let a comrade suffer like that.' He had indicated the wretch cowering against the oven, chest heaving frantically, as if his heart might burst out of his skinny ribcage at any moment. 'Surely you can do something, doc?'

The MO, grey-haired and old, had nodded wearily. 'Yes, I can do something . . . Corporal,' he had looked directly at Schulze, 'give me your pistol . . . please.'

Wordlessly, confused, half suspecting what was to come, Schulze had handed the weapon to the MO. He had fumbled with the safety catch for a moment, as if he were unfamiliar with guns, while the others had watched him mesmerized, the only sound the harsh, shallow panting of the man pinned against the oven. Then he had brought it up, aimed, and fired the very next instant at the man at the oven.

The noise had been ear-splitting. They had all jumped with shock. At the oven the injured man had given one last despairing cry before he had begun to slide down the smooth green tiles, trailing a bright red smear of blood behind him. Grimly, tears glistening in his faded old eyes, the MO had handed the pistol back to Schulze. '*Rabies*,' he had said hollowly. 'The poor wretch has been bitten by a rabid animal . . . There was no hope for him.' With that he had gone, leaving them staring at the dead man sprawled on the earthen floor like bad actors in a melodrama waiting for the curtain to go down at the end of the play.

Suddenly Schulze snapped out of his reverie and woke to their danger. 'Get back to the vehicles,' he cried frantically, 'and button down!' He aimed a wild burst at the animals. But still they came on doggedly, relentlessly, like ghost animals which could not be destroyed by any means at the disposal of human beings.

'What do you mean?' Matz yelled, unslinging his own weapon.

'What do I mean? They're frigging rabid . . . *One bite and you're a dead man*!'

And then they were running, shoving, clawing, jostling each other in their panic-stricken haste, fighting their way back to the vehicles as if the Devil himself were after them. And the dogs still came on with grim, silent purposefulness . . .

CHAPTER 6

Soon it would be dawn.

Grimly von Dodenburg pushed his helmet to the back of his head and wiped the sweat from his red-puckered brow. In front of him that lunar landscape was clearly visible in the flares that the *Amis* kept firing repeatedly ever since the failed German counter-attack.

There were dead everywhere, sprawled out on the rusting French barbed wire like bundles of abandoned rags. Shattered tree trunks poked upwards like giant tooth-picks. In one tree there lay a clump of dead *Amis*, blown up by an exploding shell, like a cluster of obscene human fruit.

All was death and destruction.

Next to him, Marchant, his head bandaged now, moodily smoking one of his cheap cigars, broke the tense, brooding pre-dawn silence. 'They are more obstinate than I would have thought, these Americans.'

'Yes,' von Dodenburg agreed drily. He had no high regard for the Americans as infantry soldiers, but the surviving paratroopers had acquitted themselves well. This night they had held off two counter-attacks by the SS and Marchant's *Milice.* Their damned two-inch mortars had proved particularly effective in breaking up the counter-attacks; the American gunners had seemed to be able to plant their deadly little bombs exactly at the points of concentration with uncanny accuracy.

Marchant looked at his watch, as somewhere a cock began to crow and to the east the sky started to flush the first ugly white of the false dawn. 'Another hour and it will be first light.' The urgency in his voice was all too obvious.

'I know, damn it!' von Dodenburg cursed miserably, feeling the first stirrings of the hot wind blowing up the Rhône valley from the south on his flushed face. He took a last angry drag at his cigarette and flung it to the ground, where it glowed a bright cherry-red. Instinctively Marchant, the policeman, thrust out his foot and crushed out the burning end. 'It is dangerous, you know, at this time of the year, with the vegetation bone-dry and the *Mistral* beginning to blow, as it is –'

'What did you say?' von Dodenburg interrupted him urgently, new hope surging through his tired body. 'What was that about the *Mistral*?'

Marchant looked at him, puzzled, and answered, 'It is the great wind that blows up the Rhône as through a funnel. It can reach speeds of . . . hm . . . one hundred kilometres, sometimes one hundred and fifty per hour. The slightest fire can be whipped up to a huge blaze by it in a matter of minutes. Each year around now we have conflagrations . . .' He broke off abruptly, for he could see that the tall handsome German was no longer listening.

Von Dodenburg's brain raced electrically as the bits and pieces of the new plan fell into place with surprising ease and swiftness. The wind was in the wrong direction, of course. It was coming from the south. But that could be taken care of. They would just have to withdraw as best they could and get behind the *Amis*. 'Marchant,' he snapped, new urgency in his voice, 'what about your wounded?' He stopped as yet another American flare burst over their heads, colouring their faces a ghastly blood-red. 'Can they all move?'

Marchant nodded. 'In the *Milice* you either move or die, when you are wounded. It is not wise to leave wounded behind to the tender mercies of that Red rabble.' He made a quick gesture as if pulling the trigger of a pistol and von Dodenburg knew instantly what the Frenchman meant. The SS had done the same in Russia. Seriously wounded men were shot by their own comrades so that they did not fall into the hands of the Ivans. SS men captured by the Russians died slowly – and horribly.

'Good. This is what I want you to do. I want you and your men to work your way around the *Amis*' left flank, and I'll do the same with my men on the right. I want no firing, avoid all trouble, until we are in position behind them. I estimate we can make it - with luck - half an hour before first light.'

The flare dropped spluttering out of the sky like a fallen angel and suddenly the two of them were blinking in the darkness. 'And what are we going to do, *Obersturmbannführer* when we are in position behind them?' Marchant asked. 'Aren't we wasting time?'

Von Dodenburg chuckled and it was not a very pretty sound. 'I shall tell you, Major. With the help of your *Mistral*, which I note is picking up in strength by the minute, we are going to start a little fire and -'

Marchant beat him to it: '*Smoke the bastards out*!' he cried excitedly.

'Exactly,' von Dodenburg answered. 'Now come on, there is not a minute to be wasted . . .'

Schulze cringed. Above him on the deck of the stalled Tiger he could hear the soft *pad-pad* of their feet. He could smell too that disgusting odour they gave off, as the marauding dogs prowled about the tanks, clawing at the metal, worrying at stanchions with their teeth, trying to find some way to get in.

'They know we're in here, you know!' Matz said in a small, tense voice, his face ashen and dripping with sweat, his nerves jingling like fiddle strings.

'Of course they do!' Schulze hissed, wiping the sweat off his face. 'They can smell us. Come on, lend a hand.' He grabbed one of the wheels which turned the turret, while Matz took the other. Grunting and straining they cranked the ten-ton turret round.

There was a sudden howl of pain and rage. They felt the long barrel of the 88mm cannon slam into something soft. Next moment there was the sound of the dog they had struck falling to the ground, where almost immediately it began attacking the tracks in savage fury, snapping and biting at them until it was exhausted and its mouth was filled with blood and broken fangs.

Almost immediately it was replaced by another of the prowling dogs, padding above their heads, making a low growling sound that made Schulze twitch with tension and apprehension, as it sought to enter the Tiger; and Schulze knew what that would mean. The rabid animal would run amok in the tight confines of the tank. Not one of them would escape its savage, dripping fangs *and that would be that*!

'You know what they're about, don't yer, Schulze?' Matz hissed huskily, a nerve completely out of control twitching at the side of his wizened face.

'Who?' Schulze asked, too preoccupied with that dreadful vision of the rabid soldier back in Russia to be able really to take in what his old comrade was saying.

'The frog-eaters. Somehow or other, they collected those crazy hounds and set them on us. Sooner or later, they're gonna hit us. Missile launchers or something like that.' He looked hard at Schulze, eyes glistening with almost unreasoning fear. 'We've got to get moving again, Schulzi, before it's too late!'

'But we can't! That shitting pile of stone is still blocking –'

He stopped short. Outside there was a sudden burst of crazy howling, mixed with screams of absolute agony and terror. Schulze flung himself to the periscope and twisted it round, as above the rabid dog dropped from the tank and raced away. In a flash, Schulze saw why. The pack had succeeded in wrenching away the thick canvas cover which was the only protection the Skoda self-propelled guns had. Now the terrified gunners were writhing back and forth on the ground in paroxysms of wild fear, being savaged by the crazed animals.

They hadn't a chance. The dogs were all over the stricken men, grunting and baying, snapping and pretending to bite each other in an attempt to ward off the competition, as their cruelly sharp fangs started ripping great hunks of blood-dripping, gory flesh from the gunners. A screaming man broke loose. Already one of his arms was gnawed to a crimson stump through which the bone gleamed a brilliant white. He staggered a few paces, screaming, screaming, screaming – and then he went down, swamped by the crazed animals, disappearing under the squirming, eager furry bodies.

'*Die, you bastards*!' Schulze shrieked hysterically and flung himself behind the turret machine-gun. He ripped off a wild burst. A dog sprang high into the air, blood jetting from the series of holes suddenly stitched the length of its grey fur like bloody button-holes, and the rest scattered out of Schulze's range. But the damage had already been done. The gunners lay there in a heap, their bodies torn and flayed to a gory mess by those cruel teeth, like the mess of offal which an awed Schulze remembered the butchers used to place before their shops for collecting before the war. With a sigh of absolute exhaustion, he let his head fall against the hard metal of the gun. Once again there was the snarl, the soft breathing, and the *pad-pad* of a dog's paws as it started to prowl on the deck above.

The minutes passed leadenly. Inside the tank there was no sound save for the hard, anxious breathing of the trapped men. From further up the stalled column there came the ripping and scratching of eager paws, trying to pull aside the tarpaulin which covered another of the Skodas, and the trapped men in the Tiger could just imagine – all too vividly – what was going through the minds of their comrades in the SP.

'God in heaven!' Schulze moaned, beating his clenched fist against the turret in impotent fury. 'There must be something we can do! *There must*!' Above, the dog was scratching away furiously with its front paws, as an ordinary dog might have done on finding a rabbit-hole. The turret was filled with its raunchy stench. Schulze gagged.

'Sergeant-Major,' a small voice said urgently.

Schulze looked down at the greasy-faced driver in his compartment. 'What is it?' he asked thickly.

'We could give each other mutual fire-support.'

'What's that supposed to mean, titty-sucker?' Schulze said to the innocent-faced youth, who was one of the new recruits from the Tyrol.

'We're protected by armour, sir, aren't we?' the youth replied. 'If each crew opened fire on the other tank or SP, they could clear the tanks of hounds in no time without any danger to themselves; then we could get out and clear –'

'*Out of the frigging mouths of frigging babes and frigging sucklings*!' Schulze roared with delight and squeezed his throat-mike hard. 'Now listen to this, you bunch of Christmas Tree soldiers . . .'

Five minutes later it was all over. On every tank deck there lay bunches of the dead animals, their fur stained and ripped by that deadly barrage. Slowly, cautiously, the crews emerged, hands gripping their pistols, ready to shoot down any animal that might still move. But there was no need to. That tremendous volume of concentrated fire had done the job all too well. Now the decks and turrets of the tanks were chipped and pocked by the bullets, a gleaming new silver against the blood red wash of the dead animals' blood.

Nose wrinkled up in repugnance, Schulze placed the tip of his boot underneath the dead dog which had plagued them and kicked it over the side, retching at its stench as he did so. On all sides the others did the same, as the ever freshening wind brought the sound of many, many marching feet their way, heralding the new danger to come.

Schulze forgot the dogs, though he would have dearly liked to strip and wash himself all over, for he itched and sweated everywhere. 'All right,' he cried at the top of his voice, as the first enemy flare sailed into the dawn sky. 'We've got five minutes! *Now let's get rid of that frigging stonefall and get on our way . . . before the frigging frog-eaters start shoving their frigging salamis up us . . .*'

CHAPTER 7

'*JABO*!'

Von Dodenburg flung a wild glance upwards. A silver, barrel-engined shape was hurtling through the dawn sky straight for them.

'*Thunderbolt*!' he cried, recognizing it immediately.

Krings, in charge of the second armoured half-track, flung himself behind the twin-barrel machine-gun and yelled wildly, 'Come on *Ami* . . . *Los*, let me tickle yer eggs for yer!' He swung the gun round to meet the challenge, as beyond the diving enemy plane von Dodenburg caught sight of the new armada of glider-towing Dakotas. The second wave was coming in. They hadn't a moment to lose.

The Thunderbolt's pilot dropped his undercarriage. Von Dodenburg, his brain racing frantically, knew why. He was using it to lower his speed. He was not going to miss this plump target: a dozen enemy half-tracks, filled with troops, spread out in completely open country without any cover. But he had not reckoned with Lieutenant Krings.

He let the Thunderbolt get within four hundred metres. Fascinated, von Dodenburg watched as the unequal duel commenced. Abruptly angry lights crackled the length of the attacking plane's wings. Vicious white and red tracer started to curve towards Krings' half-track.

'*Hit the anchors*!' the young officer yelled.

The half-track shuddered to a bone-shaking stop in a flurry of dust, its plates rattling with the shock. Next moment the Thunderbolt's slugs were stitching a crazy pattern metres away from the stalled vehicle and the silver bird was exposing its belly to a triumphant Krings, filling the whole sky at that particular moment. The lieutenant couldn't miss. He pressed the trigger, face set in a cruel, determined grin. Tracer streamed upwards. Bits of silver flew everywhere in a crazy metallic rain. Grinning wolfishly, Krings kept pouring fire into the Thunderbolt. Both wheels were sawn off. White glycol fluid started to stream from its crippled engine. The cockpit disappeared beneath the streaming liquid.

Blinded and probably dying, the pilot lost control. The stricken plane hissed above the column of half-tracks and hit the field beyond with a tremendous *crump*. There was a great rending of metal. The Thunderbolt cartwheeled, then teetered on its nose for an instant before exploding in one enormous roar that seemed to go on for ever. Almost at once a giant mushroom of thick black oily smoke started to stream upwards to the grey dawn sky while all around the shrub and parched grass began to burn.

Von Dodenburg wasted no more time. The drone of the great armada was coming ever closer. Back where the surviving Americans had gone to earth, green and red signal flares were sailing into the air to alert the pilots where the dropping zones were. It would be only a matter of minutes now. 'Do the same!' he cried, cupping his hands around his mouth. 'Everyone out . . . Light the grass . . . Come on, *dalli dalli*!'

Without waiting to see if his order was being obeyed he dropped hurriedly over the side, doubling forward, trailing the toilet roll behind him until it was exhausted. He crouched, ignoring the few stray shots coming from the nearest Americans, and clicked his lighter. It flamed at once. Protecting it from the ever-increasing wind, he touched the flame to the roll of cheap paper. It ignited immediately, and the blue flame raced along its length. On both sides the parched gorse and grass began to smoke. A gust of wind caught it. There was a sudden crackling. A soft *whoosh*. It began to burn.

Now a multitude of small fires were burning in the fields to the rear of the American positions and as the *Mistral* grew in intensity, the flames started to grow higher and higher, sweeping towards where the Americans were dug in. Now the Wotan troopers tensed like hunters waiting for the birds to rise after the beaters had done their work.

They didn't have to wait long. As the wall of flame swept down upon them, the first Americans panicked. They rose from their foxholes shouting wildly, here and there tossing away their weapons in their panic. The Wotan men and Marchant's *Milice* showed no mercy. They had suffered enough in the two counter-attacks of the night; they had a score to pay off.

Almost immediately machine-guns started to chatter and rifles began cracking away, as the Americans backed off, clearly outlined against the mounting flames. Von Dodenburg, firing with the rest, felt sorry for the retreating *Amis*. In reality they hadn't a chance. If they stuck to their positions they would be burnt alive. If they retreated into the open they would be shot down mercilessly. Now the great wall of fire was sweeping across the paras' positions at fifty kilometres an hour, devouring all in its way, a cruel fiery monster that roared and roared, leaving behind it charred grass and what looked like blackened pygmies, men who had been shrunken to half their original size by that tremendous searing heat. But von Dodenburg knew that Wotan was not out of danger yet.

Above them the second wave of American paras and glidermen circled, the pilots obviously bewildered by what was going on below. But the young colonel knew they would soon start looking for an alternative dropping zone; it would not take them long to work out which way the *Mistral* was blowing and drop their paras accordingly, away from that terrible, all-consuming blaze.

'Back to the half-tracks!' he yelled against the screams of the dying and the roar of the fires. 'Prepare to move out . . . *Move it now*!'

Almost reluctantly his young soldiers moved back. Their eyes were wild with an almost unbearable excitement and their skinny chests heaved as if they had just run a great race. Von Dodenburg recognized the symptoms. They were those of the lust of battle, an almost sexual urge to slaughter and slaughter ruthlessly, pleasurably, obscenely, until the final victim fell and they were absolutely, totally drained of energy. 'Come on!' he cried at them, angry that they should find such pleasure in the killing of their fellow human beings. Roughly he pushed them on their way, aiming kicks at men who seemed dazed or drunk, who grinned like village idiots, who mouthed meaningless sounds or cursed obscenely. '*Los*!' he yelled at them. '*Will you move your lazy, no-good arses, now*!'

Somehow or other, he and the senior NCOs managed to get them back to their half-tracks, while behind them the flames rose higher and higher and what was left of the first wave of American paras streamed towards the high ground, weapons thrown aside, all courage and will to resist spent, a completely broken force.

'*Start up*!' von Dodenburg shouted, not taking his eyes off the sinister circling Dakotas for one moment. They were very low now, perhaps two or three hundred metres, the ideal dropping height for a quick descent by well-trained men. He knew the American pilots could drop their whole load at that height within less than five minutes. Another five or so and they would be concentrated, and Wotan would have to start the whole bloody business all over again; and now in daylight, the *Amis* would have the support of their dreaded *Jabos*. They'd give the paras all the flying artillery they needed. In essence, then, he had about ten minutes to hit and wipe out the *Ami* DZ*. He bit his bottom lip until the blood came. It was going to be a damned tall order.

Schulze took in the situation at once: the burning fields; the line of half-tracks, their engines already ticking over; and beyond, at a distance of some two kilometres, well away from the blaze, the first gliders coming sailing soundlessly in, with to left and right of them parachutes opening up everywhere. 'It's the *Amis*' second wave coming in, Matzi!' he snapped and slammed his foot into the driver's shoulder.

The driver reacted immediately and the Tiger roared

* Dropping Zone

forward, throwing up a great wake of white dust as it clattered down the embankment, while Schulze pressed the button of his throat-mike and yelled: '*Mir nach – alle . . . Start firing . . . Don't let them dig in . . !*'

As the Tigers and the Skodas surged forward through the fields in a great metallic V, the machine-gunners opened up at once. Tracer zipped towards the invaders like a flight of angry red bees. Paras suddenly went limp, dead before they hit the ground. Here and there the grenades with which they were laden exploded in their webbing. Screaming helplessly, they came floating to the ground minus arms or legs.

But Schulze's main concern was the gliders. He knew that they contained the *Amis*' heavy equipment – jeeps, anti-tank guns, light mobile artillery. Once they were successfully landed, the enemy defence would harden significantly. 'Straight for the gliders, driver!' he yelled above the roar of the motors and the snap-and-crack of the wild small-arms battle.

An American para loomed up out of a ditch. He stood boldly in the path of the huge sixty-ton monster. On his shoulder he bore what a suddenly alarmed Schulze recognized as a bazooka. This latterday David was going to tackle his metal Goliath! For a moment he was too dazed to react.

Beside him, Matz raised his machine-pistol and fired a wild burst. He missed, the slugs kicking up the dirt in front of the lone American harmlessly. The para laughed. Schulze could see his perfect teeth quite clearly against his grease-blackened face. His knuckles whitened. He fired. The long tube on his right shoulder spurted angry flame. A dark projectile came hissing straight for the Tiger. It smacked into the Tiger's enormously thick glacis plate with a huge *thwack* which nearly threw Schulze off his feet. There was the stench of molten metal. For one horrifying moment Schulze thought they had been wrecked, as the motor suddenly stalled. But it was only the driver who had been rattled by the impact of the rocket and had cut his engine.

While the lone American furiously attempted to pop

another rocket into the metal tube, the driver fought to start his engine again. The driver won. The 400 HP motor sprang into ear-splitting life. The Tiger roared forward. The American saw his danger too late. His face contorted with terror as he dropped the bazooka and tried to run. Too late! The Tiger slammed into him. He gave one last terrible scream and then he was swept under those cruel tracks, his body pulped in an instant. The Tiger rolled on, leaving a flattened gory something in its wake . . .

What happened next was a confused mess of muzzle-flashes, the scrunch of metal on metal, the shriek of the ricochets and the great *whoosh* of jerricans exploding as yet another glider was hit and went up in flames. Twice Schulze heard that dread rapping of death on their turret, like the beak of some monstrous raven, as bazooka shells careened off, leaving a faint glowing redness on the inside of the turret. But in each case the *Ami* paratrooper paid for his temerity in attacking the mighty Tiger. He was mown down mercilessly, disappearing beneath those cruelly churning tracks.

Now gliders were wrecked and burning everywhere. Once they rattled past a stricken glider, its soldiers still strapped in, charred corpses trapped in what looked like a gigantic birdcage. Another time they were held up by an obstinate bazooka-man, who popped down inside the shelter of his foxhole every time they tried to hit him after firing. In the end Schulze lost his patience – the whole turret was scarred with gleaming silver holes where his rockets had struck home. He yelled above the din and racket, 'Smoke him out, driver!'

The frightened driver, who knew that the bazooka-man might well strike lucky soon, needed no urging. He raced forward to where the brave lone American crouched and braked right over his hole. Now he began to rev the tremendous engine mightily. Thick fumes poured out of the twin exhausts. Down below Schulze could imagine the trapped American ripping at his collar, gasping for breath, chest heaving frantically, eyes bulging out of his pink face until suddenly his head would tilt forward and he would be dead. 'All right, enough!' he yelled above the roar of the motors. 'He's croaked now . . . Let's get on . . .'

Quite suddenly the Americans broke. One moment they were fighting back desperately, stubbornly, in the one-sided fight, infantryman versus tank, taking casualties by the score, but still battling on valiantly as if they would never give up; the next, they were throwing their weapons away on all sides, flinging up their hands, quivering with fear and surrendering in droves, jostling and shoving each other in their eagerness to give themselves up to the triumphant Germans.

Wearily, helmet shoved to the back of his shaven skull, Schulze watched as it happened: the pleas for mercy; the offer of watches, cigarettes, wedding-rings, anything to appease the captors; the fawning smiles, the wary glances. It was always the same. Fear was infectious and it transformed men who had been brave and bold a moment before into spineless contemptible creatures, whose only thought now was not to have to die. He had seen it all before in men of all nationalities. Undoubtedly one day it would happen to him too. But for the moment, he consoled himself, he was handing out the stick, not taking it. 'All right,' he commanded his triumphant men, as they looted the survivors and the CO's half-track came rattling up through that body-littered battlefield, 'take their rings, tick-tocks and lung-torpedoes. Leave them whatever rations they may have. They're gonna need them where they're going.' Suddenly he was bored by the whole business, the dead, the destruction, the fawning prisoners, even the happy looks on the faces of his jubilant troopers. 'Keep yer peepers peeled, Matzi,' he ordered. 'I'm gonna report to the CO.'

'Like the proverbial tinned tomato,' Matz answered happily, as Schulze dropped over the side and walked over to where von Dodenburg was surveying the scene from his half-track. For a moment the two of them simply stood there, surveying the killing-ground. There were bodies everywhere, some of them already bloated with gas so that when the looters stepped on them they gave off weird little moaning sounds, as if they might still be alive and were hurt. Others crouched in ditches, caught in the act of firing, faces set in a grim suggestion of a cunning smile, as if they had thought in the instant of death that it could not happen to *them*, their glassy, unseeing eyes already covered by greedy bluebottles.

'Not a pretty sight, sir,' Schulze said, breaking the heavy oppressive silence as they watched a group of litter-bearers squelching through the gore with their stretchers, their boots blood-red up to the ankles.

Von Dodenburg nodded sombrely, eyeing a group of Americans being herded towards the rear. Broken men after one day in battle, they moved silently like sleep-walkers, heading for the cages and an uncertain future. 'Thanks, you big rogue,' he said simply. 'Thanks again.' Then he bent and without another look at the big NCO standing there in the middle of that awesome field of death he said wearily, 'All right, driver, let's go and find 19th Army HQ . . .'

For the time being the Americans had been stopped, but they would come again . . .

BOOK TWO

Frogs, Fanatics, and Fear

CHAPTER 1

Towering pillars of black smoke marked the progress of the retreat, as to the rear more and more supply dumps and depots were put to the flame. Now the columns piled up. Cars, laden with the gear of important officers, twisted in and out of the stalled lorries, honking their horns furiously. Weary foot-sloggers slumped in the ditches, their tired, worn faces lathered in sweat in the burning heat. Above, the protective fighters cruised in lazy circles, as the pilots searched the horizon for the first sign of enemy *Jabos*; for the retreating 19th Army, packed on this solitary road heading north down the valley of the River Rhône, was a bomber pilot's dream target.

General Wiese mopped his brow as they crouched there in the shade of the great dusky oaks and said, 'Well, you can see our problem, can't you, *Obersturmbannführer*? Virtually the whole of my army is retreating up this one single road from Orange through Montélimar, Valence, and then on to Lyon. It would only take one determined attack, such as that para drop yesterday, which thanks to you and your brave fellows failed, to cut us off and . . .' He stopped abruptly and shook his head like a sorely troubled man.

Opposite, two burly chain-dogs* were dragging a protesting civilian out of the column, while another two were already unslinging their carbines. Another would-be deserter had been discovered, attempting to 'take a dive', as they called it. Now his life expectancy would be numbered in minutes.

'Now the Americans are here' – Wiese stabbed the big map on his lap – 'at Avignon on the right bank of the Rhône. The French are pushing ahead of them a little, here at Pouzibacc, heading obviously for Pont St Espirit on the left bank of the

* German Military Police

river. Whether they intend to cross there and join with the Americans, I don't know. It really doesn't matter, because if we – *you*,' he looked at von Dodenburg with a wintry smile and corrected himself, 'can hold at Montélimar – here – it makes no difference at which side the main enemy advance north is made. At Montélimar the defender can dominate both sides of the River Rhône. *Klar*?'

Von Dodenburg stared earnestly at the map and said, 'Clear, sir.'

In the field opposite the would-be deserter was on his knees, wringing his hands in the classic pose of supplication, pleading to God for mercy. But God was looking the other way this burning hot August day and a hard-faced policeman was already beginning to rip the branches off the tree against which they would stand him to carry out the execution.

Wiese wrinkled his nose with distaste. 'So, *Obersturmbannführer*, it is my order that you proceed to Montélimar and prepare it for a last-ditch defence once the 19th has cleared the town. I won't be melodramatic and say "*to the last man and the last round*". But, in essence, that is what I am asking you to do. You see, it is vital that my army arrives intact for the final counter-attack there in the north. Our first – at Mortain – failed because we did not have sufficient numbers to break through to the sea. This time, the Führer wants to throw in every man available. It is imperative that the 19th should not be cut off in southern France by any link-up of their forces coming up from the south with those in the north.' In spite of the heat, the general shivered. 'That will leave us at the mercy of the Resistance. That rabble of *franc-tireurs* would slaughter us without the slightest hesitation!'

Von Dodenburg frowned. He remembered Montélimar, an undistinguished sprawl of dirty white 19th century houses dominating the road and rail network, known only for its celebrated sweetmeat. 'Nougat-Town', its inhabitants called it proudly, as if the production of that sickly candy was something to be proud of. 'It will be difficult to hold with the scant forces available to me, sir. I have already lost ten per cent of my effectives just getting here and Major Marchant of the *Milice* has suffered similar losses, I believe.'

'I know, von Dodenburg, but there is available a convalescent company, some two hundred strong, of the SS Charlemagne Division. I am going to place that under your command.' He looked hopefully at the younger officer.

Across the road, the policemen had tied the sobbing prisoner's hands behind his back and were pushing him towards the tree. He had broken down completely. His pants were soiled and the tears were streaming down his ashen face.

Von Dodenburg pursed his lips and said slowly. 'It'll be a tall order, some twelve hundred men, plus a dozen armoured vehicles or so, trying to hold a medium-sized town against a whole army.'

Wiese rose to his feet and handed the map to a waiting staff officer. He forced a smile. '*Obersturmbannführer* von Dodenburg, I have heard a great deal of the exploits of SS Assault Regiment Wotan in this war. If anyone can hold the Americans, it will be your regiment. *Hals und Beinbruch*!'*

Von Dodenburg clicked to attention, telling himself it was always the same when senior officers gave impossible orders. They always flattered you. He grinned slightly and wondered how many brave fools in this war had allowed themselves to be flattered into an early death.

Across the way, a big red-faced MP had stuffed the deserter's mouth full of earth and grass to stop him screaming. Wiese nodded his approval and, raising his gloved hand to his cap in salute, he turned and walked to his waiting car rapidly, as if he couldn't get away soon enough. A minute later, with his driver honking his horn furiously, he had disappeared into the column.

'*FEUER*!' the burly MP sergeant yelled. Von Dodenburg jumped, startled, but the shuffling wrecks of Wiese's infantry did not even turn. They were past caring. Bowed with fatigue, their uniforms soaked with sweat and powdered with

* Roughly 'happy landings'

white dust, they shambled on ever northwards, dragging their hopeless, battle-drugged bodies as if heavy weights were tied to each ragged leg.

Von Dodenburg frowned. At the tree the MPs were hanging a crude sign around the dead man's neck. It read: '*This is the fate of all defeatists, deserters and cowards*!' For him at that moment the dead deserter symbolized the whole of the retreating 19th Army. Discipline and order were breaking down. Panic was in the air. Now it seemed that everything depended upon his pathetic handful of veteran SS men, his greenbeaks, and his strange new allies, the French. Von Dodenburg shook his head ruefully as he began to walk back slowly to his half-tracks. It was going to be a tall order, a very tall order indeed. Behind him the dead man began to rotate slowly in the heightening *Mistral* . . .

But if von Dodenburg was dismayed by the conditions of the 19th Army's retreat, Schulze and Matz were delighted. Only half an hour before, as they had rolled up in the Tiger to take up flank guard on the side road bordering *Route Nationale* Seven, they had come across an abandoned *Wehrmacht* cart stacked with French champagne, theirs for the taking. In that burning heat they had needed no second invitation to drink the stuff. As a delighted Schulze had proclaimed to Matz, similarly guzzling the fine wine, 'I prefer retreats to advances, old house. You get a better kind of piss. *Prosit*!'

Now as the horse-drawn cart, filled with giggling, obviously drunken women, hove into sight where Schulze had positioned the Tiger, he added to that immortal wisdom with an uproarious, 'And a better class of gash, as well!' He breathed out fervently, a look of awe on his face, as he took in the gaily dressed women in the *Wehrmacht* cart, who were obviously whores working for the 19th Army. 'Willya feast yer optics on that Matzi – *real hot steaming female gash on the hoof*!'

Hurriedly the big NCO tossed away his bottle of champagne, spat on a hand as big as a steam-shovel, smoothed down his cropped hair and dropped hastily to the ground. Gallantly he bowed and chortled, as the sway-backed nag came to a halt, twin jets of steam coming from its nostrils with the effort, '*Bonjour, mesdames. Comment allez-vous?*'

A big blonde whore, whose enormous breasts threatened to burst out of the tight confines of her blouse at any moment, pulled a fat finger out of her ear, eyed the wax deposited there, and said in the accent of Berlin-Wedding*, 'Frigging Russkis, girls!' She sighed wearily as if she were sorely tried. 'And you know what they're like when you have to service 'em. Frigging fiddler's elbows!' Absent-mindedly she stuffed her left breast back into her blouse, for the sigh had dislodged the enormous globe of white flesh.

Schulze's eyes bulged at the sight of that tremendous dug. He twisted his head to one side, face suddenly crimson, unable to speak for a moment until finally he croaked, like a man who was being slowly strangled, 'But you're German!'

'Of course, we're frigging German!' the blonde retorted. 'Not that we don't talk a little French now and agen, if you get my meaning.' She winked naughtily, while the others burst into drunken laughter at this witty sally.

'Oh, I get it all right,' Schulze breathed, '*that I do*!'

Behind, an eager Matz and the rest of the Tiger crew were already lining up, eyes eager and expectant, their Tiger abandoned, the war forgotten *now*.

Recovering a little from his shock, Schulze said with a winning smile, 'I wonder if the ladies would not like to relax for a little while? In those bushes over there? I'spect you find this French sun rather . . . er . . . tiresome.'

Behind him Matz farted loudly and said scornfully, 'Get a load o' him? *Tiresome* indeed. Oh my frigging migraine!'

'Don't be so frigging coarse when you're in the presence of real frigging ladies,' Schulze chided him, not taking his eyes off the large whore descending from the cart somewhat clumsily to reveal that she was minus her knickers. Up front

* A district of Berlin

the tired old field-grey of a driver whipped the ancient nag frantically, as its hooves flailed the air and it was threatening to be lifted from its feet by the weight of the whore.

'Get down, damn yer,' he cried, 'get down . . . And you, fat Lisa, take it a bit easier on old Bertha, she ain't what she used to be.'

'Frig Bertha!' the fat whore said easily, 'I'm in a hurry.' Urgently she flung herself into an awed Matz's arms. Nearly knocked off his feet by that tremendous weight, he gasped in awestruck disbelief at his own good fortune. 'My God, it'll be just like climbing Everest!' Next moment he had disappeared into the bushes with Lisa.

One by one the eager soldiers slipped away with the excited drunken whores and soon the bushes echoed with sighs of ecstasy, cries of delight and an occasional moan as some sex-starved soldier cried, 'Oh, catch me quick . . . I think it's gonna croak me . . . *Oh, oh, oh* . . !'

It was while they were thus so delightfully occupied that it happened. Sergeant Schulze, his pants pulled down around his jackboots, red-faced, groaning and sweating with the effort, suddenly felt something long and hard poked against his naked buttocks.

Carried away by the sheer delight of his current activity, he deigned not to notice its importuning for a few moments; naturally he had other things on his mind. But the poking persisted. 'Oh, frigging well knock off the joking, Matzi!' he grunted angrily, while below him the whore wriggled with pleasure, thinking that his running-mate was up to one of his old tricks. 'If you can't frigging well do it, fuck off and let *mee*!' He yelped as that hard prodding suddenly became very painful.

He faltered in his stroke and below him the whore tightened her grip on him, as if afraid he might leave her at this crucial moment, which unfortunately was to be the case. Spitting fire, he craned his head round, ready to 'make a sow' of the unfortunate Matz, as he would have phrased it.

But there would be no 'sow-making' this particular hot August afternoon. For standing there was a short-panted barefoot boy, face red with flushed embarrassment at what was taking place on the ground, pointing a rifle as big as himself at him. Behind him stood other similarly-clad youths, equally embarrassed at the sight of this mass coupling. But if they were embarrassed, there was no mistaking the grim intent in their eyes and the threatening manner in which they held their ancient rifles.

Slowly, miserably slowly, Schulze felt that delightful pillar of hard flesh disappear, even though below him the whore, her eyes tightly screwed together as if she wished to blot out all sight, all sound, pounded away. But it was no use. Lying there, literally 'caught with my skivvies down', as he would have told it to his cronies in the sergeants' mess, Sergeant Schulze began to raise his hands. With a sinking, helpless feeling, he knew he had just become a prisoner of the *maquis* . . .

CHAPTER 2

Abbé, Comte Pierre du Pres was the strangest SS officer that Kuno von Dodenburg had ever encountered in his long career with the Armed SS; and in his time he had met some very strange ones. With his empty left sleeve tucked into his belt, the black shade over his left eye and belt stuffed with grenades, he was all warrior. But with the silver crucifix of a chaplain opposite the tarnished stars of his rank, his tonsured head, and gentle, all-understanding manner, he could be nothing else but some provincial aristocratic priest, which, of course, he was.

'From St Cyr, *Obersturmbannführer*, I went straight into the priesthood,' he had explained in that soft-spoken manner of his some five minutes before. 'In Thirty-nine I answered the call immediately. My old regiment, you know, the *Chasseurs*. But the rot had set in even there . . . I was glad when the great crusade against the Godless, heathen bolsheviks was called by your Führer in forty-two. It gave me a new purpose in life – to fight against those who threatened our western Christian culture. I volunteered at once, of course.'

'Of course,' von Dodenburg had echoed, somewhat overwhelmed by this strange combination of priest and warrior; and there was no denying there was a great deal of the latter in his make-up. The orders and decorations which covered his skinny chest, plus the Knight's Cross of the Iron Cross dangling from his throat, were proof enough that he had seen his share of combat on the eastern front fighting the 'Godless, heathen bolsheviks', as he called the 'Ivans'.

Now as the retreating 19th Army streamed by the old farmhouse which stank of stale cabbage and sweat, von Dodenburg expounded his plans to du Pres and Marchant: 'We move to Montélimar tonight. General Wiese has given us priority number one as far as road traffic is concerned.' Von

Dodenburg laughed hollowly. 'And it is pretty obvious from what you see out there, no one in the 19th is going *southwards* any more.'

Marchant took his cheap cigar out of his mouth. 'You can say that again, *Obersturmbannführer*,' he grunted sourly. 'Now it's going to be up to Frenchmen to defend their own country against the Americans.'

The warrior-priest sniggered. 'How curious life is, *mon fils*. Frenchmen fighting their *liberators* on behalf of their *oppressors*. How droll!'

Von Dodenburg ignored these comments. 'In my eyes, none of us is fighting for a nationalist cause any more. All of us, German, French, Dutch, Polish, Belgian - and all the rest of the nationalities now fighting in the ranks of the Greater German Army - are fighting for a European ideal against the evil of communism.' Even as he spouted the new propaganda line, von Dodenburg felt an absolute hypocrite. Germany was fighting for naked survival, and desperately needed these renegades, traitors, idealists, call them what you will, to continue that desperate fight. He smiled winningly at his two allies and snapped, 'Let us now concentrate on the task at hand. Darkness will protect us from the attentions of the enemy *Jabos*, thank God. However, by the same token it will slow down our progress. But we must urge our drivers to maximum effort. We must reach Montélimar by dawn! From what I have heard, the garrison there is decidedly shaky. At the first sight of the Americans they might well run, and that would naturally destroy all our hopes of being able to defend the place.'

'We might have trouble with the *maquis*,' Marchant warned sombrely. 'Now that you Germans are pulling back, the rats will be coming out of their holes everywhere and it is two hundred long kilometres to Montélimar.'

'*D'accord*,' du Pres agreed and said in that gentle manner of his, 'But the problem is easily solved, *mon Commandant*. Fight fire with fire. At the first sign of trouble on the part of the gentlemen of the Resistance, we take hostages and burn down a village or two. I think that should suffice, don't you?' He smiled sweetly.

At any other time von Dodenburg would have burst into disbelieving laughter. How could a man of the cloth be so bloodthirsty? But time *was* running out and he could not dwell on the peculiarities of human nature. Instead he snapped, 'Yes, I am afraid that is the way it has to be – fight fire with fire. Now this is going to be our order of march . . .'

But von Dodenburg did not get far in his detailed plan of the night's march south. Outside, the lazy, hot afternoon stupor was ripped apart by the roar of a motorcycle in a hurry. Von Dodenburg looked up angrily from his maps. It was Lieutenant Krings, his uniform caked with white dust, a dark red trickle of blood running down his face, his eyes blazing angrily. He let the machine drop even before it had ceased running and thrusting up his goggles, he doubled towards the farmhouse.

Von Dodenburg flung open the door for him. 'Where's the fire, Krings?' he demanded, knowing instinctively that something serious had gone wrong.

'It's Sergeant Schulze, sir!' Krings gasped, gratefully accepting the brilliant-white linen handkerchief an anxious du Pres had handed him to stem the flow of blood from his temple.

'What about Schulze?'

'He's gone, together with his Tiger and the rest of the crew,' Krings answered miserably.

'Gone . . . gone where?' von Dodenburg stuttered. 'You mean he's deserted?'

'No, sir,' Krings answered. 'Those shits of the *maquis* have got them – and the tank. I went out on the bike on routine inspection of our perimeter as you ordered, sir, and found them missing from their post. There were obvious signs of a scuffle, but no dead or anything like that. They wanted that Tiger and they didn't slaughter Schulze and his people because obviously –'

'Only our people could drive it.'

'Exactly, sir. Well, the trail of the Tiger wasn't difficult to follow and I followed it to the hamlet of Hauterives, some ten kilometres from the *Route Nationale*. It was there I came under concentrated fire and got this.' He touched his wounded temple gingerly, while du Pres tut-tutted soliticiously. 'I thought it better to break off and report to you.'

'Quite right too,' von Dodenburg answered, his mind racing frantically, trying to sort out this new situation, one that might well throw the timing of their night march into complete disarray.

Marchant seemed to read his thoughts for he said brutally, 'They're as good as dead anyway, *Obersturmbannführer*. SS in the hands of that Red rabble . . .' He spat on the floor and drew a dirty finger under his throat, as if he were slitting it with a sharp knife.

Du Pres shook his head as if in disapproval, but said nothing.

Krings, for his part, bit his lip as if to prevent himself from blurting out a plea for help, but his eyes were eloquent with their appeal for von Dodenburg to do something.

The young colonel made his decision. 'I have no intention of allowing my men to be slaughtered by the partisans in cold blood. It's my guess that the people who kidnapped them will keep them alive until they have taught the partisans how to operate the Tiger. That will take some time. Perhaps most of this day. So we act immediately. An all-out attack by your *Milice*, Marchant, your men of the Charlemagne, du Pres, and my own chaps. There is no time to be lost. We must catch the partisans on the rebound. We'll plan as we go along. Come on,' he said grabbing for his helmet, '*los . . . move it*!'

They 'moved it', and Krings gasped a sigh of relief, the gratitude all too obvious on his young face.

They had thrown the rope above the branch of the nearest plane tree so that each end of it finished in a noose around the neck of the cowed deserters from the 19th Army. Beforehand the grinning young Resistance men in their shabby blue overalls and tattered white plimsolls had stripped them naked and lashed their arms behind their backs. Now they slipped the nooses around each man's neck and arranged the rope in such a way that while one man was hanging, the other deserter could just touch the ground with the tips of his bare toes. So they jerked up and down in a macabre see-saw, a sadistic dance of death, being egged and cheered on by the flushed young men, each terrified German trying to postpone the inevitable and by taking the weight on his toes, only to be throttled once more as his comrade in misery found the pressure on his neck unbearable and kicked out in his turn to continue the balancing act. Both deserters, grotesquely enough, as is customary in cases of strangulation, had stout purple erections.

Further up the tree-covered *place*, where before the war the old men had played their *boule* in the cool of the evening and the young ones had drunk their *rouge* and eyed the strolling girls, they were shaving the heads of the naked whores, finishing off in a burst of laughter as they painted a large black swastika on each pair of plump buttocks. Hardened as they were after years of servicing soldiers on half a dozen fronts, this last act of mindless cruelty had broken the whores' spirits. Now as the yelling, contemptuous young men pushed the shaven-headed, naked girls into the dust, they lay there sobbing hysterically, as if their very hearts were broken.

'What a bunch of cruel shits!' Schulze hissed out of the side of his mouth to Matz, who like himself was tied to the side of the burning hot Tiger, which now held pride of place in the *maquis* village, its turret already adorned with the red, white and blue flash of the Resistance, while a *tricoleur* hung limply from the opening.

'Why don't they frigging croak us and have it over with?' Matz asked through cracked swollen lips, his eyes black and narrowed to slits where they had punched and beaten him an hour before.

'Because they need us,' Schulze answered, not taking his

eyes off the sadistic scene for a minute, as if he were trying to commit every single cruel detail to memory. 'They need us to show the pricks how to run the battle-wagon, once they've had a bellyful of their little games.'

'And then?'

Schulze opened his mouth to answer, but stopped short. One of the two naked men had slumped. His companion's face went a brilliant red. Frantically he twisted and turned his head, eyes bulging crazily, tongue hanging out of the side of his tortured mouth like a piece of bright red leather. To no avail! His head dropped to one side, too, that grotesque erection shrinking slowly: he was dead as well.

Schulze licked his parched, blood-caked lips and said, 'They've snuffed it. It won't be long now and they'll come for us.'

'What then?' Matz whispered, his fear all too apparent.

Schulze put a bold face on it, for the sake of his old comrade. 'Don't cream yer skivvies, Matzi,' he said defiantly, as one of the young *maquis* forced a hysterically sobbing Lisa to her feet and, coming up from behind the naked whore, held up her enormous breasts for the benefit of another *maquis* who began to take pictures of them with his camera. 'We ain't snuffed it yet. Just look at the way that pig is handling Lisa's milk factory. Christ on a crutch, if I only had my flippers free, why I'd rip off his stupid turnip and stuff it up his own arsehole!'

Matz did not seem to hear that terrible threat. Instead a new light of hope started to creep into his battered eyes and he said after a moment, as the laughing *maquis* now forced the hysterical whore onto her knees, with her enormous buttocks raised in the air, 'If they want us to learn them how to use the Tiger, they'll have to untie our flippers, won't they, Schulze?'

Schulze nodded, broad face burning with frustrated rage at the indignities now being heaped on the helpless whore, 'Yes, natch!'

'Well,' Matz said slowly, 'how many of the pricks can get in the driving seat with me, eh?'

'*Am I Jesus Christ?*' Schulze snorted. 'One, I suppose.'

'That's what I suppose as well, comrade. And if I have my hands free and there's only one of them in the driving compartment with me,' Matz paused, his battered face suddenly mean and cruel, 'I'm gonna fucking run amok . . . and then those sadistic pricks will see just what it's like to be at the receiving end of sixty tons of solid Krupp steel . . . oh yes they will.' He leaned back against the tank, his mind made up, suddenly a very contented man.

CHAPTER 3

The *maquis* were amateurs, von Dodenburg could see that as he surveyed the hamlet through his glasses. Set on a hilltop, naked save for the olive groves to the right, the place was an ideal site for defence. But what sentries they had posted lolled in the shade of the buildings on the outskirts, instead of being dug in on the slope. He swung up the glasses and surveyed the church tower, topped as was customary in this part of France with a skeletal iron construction.

Next to him du Pres did the same. 'No look-out up there. How fortunate for us that the Godless pack never visit the church,' he sniggered softly.

'How fortunate indeed.' Von Dodenburg took another look at the giant hulk of the Tiger squatting in the burning square and lowered his glasses. 'All right, they are still alive and apparently their captors have no idea we are here. The *Mistral* must have drowned any sound we might have made getting here. Now it will have to be a straightforward infantry attack. The clatter of the tanks and half-tracks would alarm them too soon.'

Du Pres nodded his agreement and said, 'By now Marchant's *Milice* must be in position over there in the olives.'

'I would think so. We, however, must get as close as possible to the far end of the village to seal off any escape route. As soon as the balloon goes up when Marchant attacks, we make a rush for it – up that track at ten o'clock. Got it?'

'Got it, *Obersturmbannführer*!. du Pres snapped, all soldier now, iron in his voice.

'I want to get so close when the trouble starts that they can't indulge themselves in any last-minute slaughter of the prisoners.'

Du Pres laughed softly and it was not a pleasant sound. 'No, they won't do that if they think they're going to be captured. They'll be hoping to save their precious skins.' His one eye gleamed evilly and he added, 'Unfortunately that is going to remain a pious hope – for them. Fight fire with fire, do you remember, *Obersturmbannführer*? I think the time has come to give the *maquis* a little display of pyrotechnics. It might keep them nice and quiet for a little while, *hein*?'

Almost sadly von Dodenburg agreed. 'Yes, I suppose it is time for a show of force. *There will be no prisoners taken*! Pass the word to your men. I will do the same with mine. Now,' he snapped, driving the thought of the massacre to come out of his mind, 'let us get on with the most important business – the rescuing of my poor fellows . . .'

Matz flashed Schulze a knowing look as the skinny Frenchman in his ragged overalls squeezed by them in the crowded turret and squirmed his way into the driving compartment. Schulze winked solemnly and flexed his big muscles. Next to him the bearded *maquis*, his belt filled with grenades, pistols and knives, growled, '*Sale con*!' and pushed him roughly. Hastily Schulze lowered his head so that the Frenchman could not see the burningly angry look in his eyes.

With difficulty Matz squirmed into the driving seat, his every move watched by the skinny Frenchman, who stank of garlic and grease; Matz guessed he was some sort of mechanic from the smell. Probably he had been chosen to learn to drive the Tiger because of his technical training. 'Don't worry, frog-eater,' a little voice within him snarled, 'you'll never drive this battle-wagon, if Frau Matz's handsome son has anything to do with it.'

Now in a series of grunts in broken German and a lot of dumbshow, Matz took the Frenchman through the Tiger's very complicated gear system, watching the latter's eyes widen when he realized that the sixty-ton monster had nearly thirty different gears.

'*Comprenez*?' he asked, not caring whether the 'frog-eater' understood or not, only concerned whether he would be able to start the engines and get the Tiger moving. Of course, the Frenchman was armed. He had a British sten-gun hanging from his shoulder, but in the tight confines of the driving compartment that wouldn't help him much. 'I'll ram it right up his skinny arse till his eyes pop!' Matz hissed to himself in pleasurable anticipation, his hand already twitching, eager to turn on the big engines.

Above in the turret, surrounded by at least six of the partisans, who were staring inside awed and open-mouthed like a set of village yokels, Schulze was demonstrating how the turret moved, hand cranking it around effortlessly. There were cries of delight as one of them sitting on the mighty 88mm cannon swung round with it. '*Oh la la*!' they cried. '*C'est tres joli*!'

'Like frigging kids on the merry-go-round!' Matz told himself scornfully.

Next to him the skinny partisan pointed at the starter. '*Marchez*?' he demanded.

'Move?' Matz echoed eagerly, finger itching to press it. He licked his cracked lips. '*Ja . . . ja* . . .mar . . . anyway, whatever you said, you frog streak of piss!'

The Frenchman frowned, while Matz waited tensely, heart thumping away with excitement. *Would the prick never make his decision*?

The skinny Frenchman puffed out his hollow cheeks in the Gallic fashion and decided. '*Allez – roulez*!' he commanded, gaze fixed almost hypnotically on the controls so that he missed the sudden look of triumph that flashed across Matz's battered face.

Matz didn't give him a chance to change his mind. He hit the button. The *Maibach* engines burst into life immediately, first go. Matz forced himself to take his time, although he was trembling all over with suppressed excitement. He revved the engine carefully. The noise rose to a crescendo. Above, the Frenchmen gasped and yelled at the racket. Secretly Schulze touched Matz's skinny shoulder with his boot. He knew what the little man was up to.

Matz said a silent prayer that the engine wouldn't stall on him now. He flung a last glance through the narrow driving slit. Not fifty metres away there was the solid stone wall of the little church. That would do nicely, he told himself, and began to let out the clutch gingerly. Next to him the *maquis* had not noticed anything. 'Frog-eater, you're gonna have the father and mother of a frigging headache in half a mo'!' Matz promised himself gleefully. He let the clutch out fully.

With a rusty creak, the sixty-ton monster lurched forward. Swiftly Matz flung her through ten forward gears and the tank started to gather speed. The church wall was only twenty-five metres away now. Next to him the *maquis* continued to gawp. Unsuspecting as he was, he still did not notice the thick centuries-old church wall looming up ever closer; he was too intent on the controls. Matz braced himself and put his foot down harder.

Suddenly the *maquis* became aware of the danger, as he flashed a look through the slit on his side. '*Arrêtez, sale con*!' he yelled. '*Le mûr*!'

'*Frig off . . . piss in the wind*!' Matz chortled and pressed his foot down even harder.

Next to him the *maquis* fumbled frantically with his sten. But in the tight confines of the wildly swaying tank, it was difficult to free the little machine-pistol. Now the wall filled their vision. They were heading for it at twenty kilometres an hour. Above, the men on the turret yelled in alarm. Someone loosed off a wild shot. Schulze ducked beneath the cover of the shield, big hands seeking the co-axial machine-gun. A *maquis* aimed at his head with the butt of his Mauser. Schulze ducked at the very last moment and the brass-shod butt struck his shoulder. He howled with pain, but still he found the trigger. Someone loosed off a burst of sten fire. Matz yelled wildly and then it happened. The Tiger struck the wall at full tilt. The *maquis* next to Matz, fumbling frantically for his weapon, slammed forward against the metal. His nose burst with an audible crack. Bright-red blood jetted from his nose and for a moment he leaned there helplessly, moaning. Matz didn't give him a chance to recover. He grabbed the spanner next to him and cracked it down on the man's skull. He went limp immediately with a soft moan, unconscious or dead, Matz did not know or care.

Hastily he flung the Tiger into reverse. With a rumble of falling masonry and the rending of torn metal, the sixty-ton monster backed off, throwing the man who was about to toss a grenade into the open turret off balance. He didn't get a second chance. Schulze slammed the turret shut and loosed off a wild burst.

In an instant all was wild confusion. Everywhere the startled, angered *maquis* started firing. An evil-looking bearded giant ripped a salvo the length of the wall where the other Tiger crew-members were lined up. They went down in a flurry of flying limbs, red button-holes stitched the length of their bodies. They were dead before they hit the ground. Another *maquis* lobbed a grenade towards the sobbing, naked whores grouped around the ancient nag. Its explosion tore the head off the unfortunate horse, hosing their naked bodies with bright, steaming crimson blood. They went into hysterics again.

But it was the Tiger that received most of their attention, as Matz flung it into a series of wild manoeuvres, breaking left and right in a flurry of white dust in the tight confines of the square, trying to find an exit, knowing that time was running out. It took only some brave fool armed with a sticky bomb to run forward and clamp the anti-tank device against their side and that would be that. Above in the turret, well aware of that dreaded possibility, Schulze hosed the streets to left and right, praying fervently that the machine-gun wouldn't jam. For if it did, they would be finished; and this time the enraged frog-eaters would show no mercy . . .

*

Von Dodenburg waited no longer, as the wild firing broke out in the hilltop village and Marchant's green signal-flare hissed into the leaden sky above the olives. '*Attack . . . attack*!' he yelled and shrilled madly on his whistle. Everywhere his men rose from their hiding places with a great cheer.

To his right, du Pres made the sign of the cross over the bent, helmeted heads of his troopers and then without hesitation scuttled forward, crying, '*Vive la France . . ! Pour Dieu et le Paix*!'

Now the men of the mixed Franco-German attack streamed upwards on three sides, firing as they ran, yelling like madmen, oblivious to the first ragged fire coming their way kicking up the dust in angry little spurts at their flying feet.

A *maquis* popped up out of a hole, sten-gun at the ready. Von Dodenburg's cruelly shod boot lashed out - he had no time to fire - and connected with his unshaven chin. His spine cracked audibly and he went reeling backwards without a sound, gun tumbling from suddenly nerveless fingers. Behind von Dodenburg a greenbeak stuck his bayonet into the dying man. With a grunt he heaved it out again. There was a terrible sucking sound. The blade came out gleaming with red blood.

They raced up to the first houses. Du Pres's grenadiers were veterans. A grenade through the window. A heavy foot slammed against the frail door. A vicious burst of machine-pistol fire into the interior. Then the crazy rush inside, firing from the hip as they ran. No one came out . . .

Snipers were operating up in the windows of the houses leading into the chaotic square. Here and there the leading attackers stumbled, rifles dropping from their sweating hands, falling flat without a sound; going down stubbornly, moaning as they did so, like boxers refusing to give up; dropping startled, staring at their shattered limbs, eyes full of utter disbelief, as if this couldn't be happening to *them*.

For a moment they bunched. But not for long. '*Flame-throwers*!' von Dodenburg yelled angrily, standing in the centre of the dusty street, ignoring the slugs cutting the air all around him. '*Where are those shitting flame-throwers*?'

A tall gangling youth came up panting, a heavy pack bouncing up and down on his skinny shoulders. 'Here I am, sir,' he said in the thick accents of the South Tyrol, ducking instinctively as the snipers began to concentrate their fire on him; for already they had recognized the round pack and the dread weapon it supplied.

'You and you,' von Dodenburg cried to the riflemen sheltering in the nearest doorway, 'cover him . . . Now off you go!'

The trio set off at an awkward lope. Von Dodenburg raised his Schmeisser and began ripping off angry but controlled bursts to left and right, aiming at the upper windows where the snipers were hidden. Glass shattered. Someone screamed shrilly. A window burst and a body came flying through it to slam to the ground below like a sack of wet cement.

The first of the escort dropped cursing, bright-red blood jetting out of his shattered knee. Von Dodenburg felt a slug hammer against his helmet and he reeled back against the wall, suddenly dizzy and sick. The South Tyrolean cursed and faltered for an instant. A slug had slammed into his left arm. The old hare at his side yelled in sudden alarm, '*Keep moving or you'll fry us to a frigging cinder*!'

The flame-thrower operator stumbled on, blood streaming down his brawny arm. Then he stopped, legs braced apart like a western gunslinger in some movie shoot-out. A moment's pause. He pressed the trigger. There was a sound like some primeval monster taking a fiery breath. A stream of blue-tinged oily flame shot out and upwards. Like a rod it slapped the windows to the right. Almost immediately the paint began to bubble and blister. There was a stench of burning. Von Dodenburg wrinkled up his nostrils in disgust. Next moment a flaming, writhing torch which was a man came falling from the nearest window to slam into the cobbles, tossing and turning, vainly trying to slap out the rising flames with hands that were themselves aflame. Now they started to move forward once more, the big gangling youth flaming the buildings to left and right.

Machine-gun fire came hissing from a squat concrete building to the left, which von Dodenburg had first taken for a barn. Now he realized it was one of the strongpoints which the German Todt Organisation* had built before the enemy invasion of the south of France.

Almost immediately the flame-thrower operator wreathed it with angry flame. Once, twice, three times. To no avail! The bunker had been too carefully constructed for the flames to reach the *maquis* inside. Von Dodenburg didn't hesitate. Beyond, glimpsed through the drifting smoke and glare of explosives, he could see the lone *maquis* trailing the Tiger which was vainly trying to bull its way out of the *place* down one of the narrow streets. His men didn't have long to live. He darted forward, slugs from an enemy machine-gun erupting in angry blue flashes all around his flying feet. He slammed into the nearside wall, dull-red and glowing still from the flame-thrower. Inside he could hear excited chatter. A rifle poked its way out of a loop-hole just above his head and began snapping off single shots. Obviously they hadn't spotted him.

Von Dodenburg drew a deep breath. He snapped another full magazine into his machine-pistol. With his other hand, he drew his last grenade from his boot. 'March or die,' Marchant had warned. Well this was certainly 'march or die'. He pulled the pin and lobbed the grenade inside. '*One . . . two . . . three*!' He counted the seconds off urgently, while machine-gun bullets chipped the concrete all about him, stinging his face with the sharp particles. A muffled *crump*. A shriek of absolute agony. Thick black smoke billowed from

* German military labour unit

the entrance. With a roar von Dodenburg went in, machine-pistol chattering.

The place stank of garlic and unwashed bodies. Gasping and choking in the smoke-filled gloom, half-blinded by the fumes, von Dodenburg sprang over the shattered bodies and the moaning men on the floor. He swung round the corner. Illuminated by a hissing petroleum lamp, he saw a dead man slumped over a wrecked table. Was he the last one? Von Dodenburg's eyes flickered restlessly from side to side. In this kind of fighting, he knew, one second's hesitation and you were a dead man.

A sudden whimpering. He spun round, his nerves almost gone. To his left there was another dark passage leading off from the main bunker. He ripped the pin out of his last grenade and lobbed it down the passage. Hastily he flung himself against the wall, face turned away. A thick grunt, a wave of acrid fumes and the blast hit him like a blow from a wet, pudgy fist. Then he was spraying the passage from left to right viciously, the slugs howling off the walls.

A round British grenade rolled towards him, spluttering angrily. He kicked it back instinctively and ducked. *Nothing*! The grenade had failed to explode. He sprang forward. A man dying on the floor tried to grab his ankles. He lashed out. The *maquis* screamed and reeled back, blood spurting from ears and shattered nose. He darted round the bend, nerves racing like trip-hammers. The Schmeisser chattered viciously. Slugs howled off both sides of the chamber, striking up angry little spurts of blue flame, the noise ear-splitting, chipped-off concrete flying everywhere, stinging his taut, flushed face like the bites of giant mosquitoes. By an effort of sheer will-power he tore his finger from the trigger. He was wasting bullets. The occupants of the chamber, which was obviously the *maquis* command post, were already dead or dying: a macabre tableau of total war, the bodies shattered and flayed by his bullets and the grenades, as if some crazy butcher had gone to work with a blunt knife.

Suddenly von Dodenburg was overcome by nausea. He

couldn't help himself. He began to retch and retch, his shoulders heaving frantically. Blindly he staggered outside into the bright sunlight, into the wildly cheering throng, and collapsed . . .

CHAPTER 4

The firing was beginning to die away now. Here and there a rifle cracked, or there was the short swift burst of a machine-pistol. Occasionally there was a high-pitched hysterical scream, as they hounded another woman out of the houses (the men had all been slaughtered) and shot her as she ran. Already at the far end of the hill village, Marchant's *Milice* were putting the houses to fire, the *Mistral* turning the flames into a blaze in an instant.

Von Dodenburg wiped the sweat off his forehead with the back of his arm and stared as Schulze drew the tarpaulin over the three dead Tiger men. A little way off, the whores had been calmed at last and under du Pres's disapproving gaze they were looting the houses in an attempt to find something to cover their gross bodies.

Schulze saluted and said, 'Thanks, sir. I thought our goose was cooked that time - really up to our hooters in crap!'

Von Dodenburg nodded sombrely. He didn't like what had been done here. It was a war crime, he knew that; but then, he tried to console himself, all war is a crime. 'Pick yourself a couple of new gunners and a radio operator from the panzer grenadiers.' He flashed a quick look at the sky. The sun was already beginning to sink. Soon it would be dark and he wanted to be on his way by then. 'We march south as soon as this business is taken care . . .' He broke off and turned to stare at the ragged barefoot boy that du Pres's SS men were bringing in, his face already swollen and rapidly turning black where they had beaten him.

Naturally the kid was afraid - he was trembling all over - but there was a look of defiance in his dark eyes and his lips were clamped tightly together in a stubborn, wilful manner. He might have been seven years old and von Dodenburg could see he had all the makings of a *maquis*. And yet . . .

Du Pres seemed to be able to read his mind, for he said in that gentle understanding way of his, acquired from years of listening to rural peccadillos in the confessional, 'What is he to be, *Obersturmbannführer*?'

'What do you mean – *what is he to be*?'

'Should he be allowed to live and relate what happened here?' du Pres persisted, voice as gentle as ever. 'Should he be the one who will make heroes and martyrs for *la belle France* out of the Red rabble?' He indicated the dead bodies sprawled everywhere among the bullet-pocked houses. Suddenly there was iron in the former priest's voice: 'Or should the little wretch die, an unknown, just another casualty, one of many millions in this long war, taking his knowledge, his secrets with him?' He looked hard at the tall SS officer. 'It is your decision, sir. Martyr for France – or just another piece of cannonfodder? For remember this, *Obersturmbannführer*: if that boy survives, it will be he and his like who will write the history of the Third Reich. Through his eyes the world will see and interpret your vaunted New Order.' He looked challengingly at von Dodenburg and suddenly the latter realized how much they were pawns in the history of the Second World War. The truth about them, all of them fated to die violently before it was over, would be the truth the survivors were prepared to give.

Von Dodenburg nodded slowly. 'Yes,' he whispered huskily, hearing his own voice as if it were coming from a million kilometres away. 'You are right, du Pres. Deal with him.'

The ex-priest smiled benignly at the ragged boy. 'I shall give you the General Absolution,' he said softly, as the two SS Charlemagne troopers cocked their rifles. 'Close your hands, boy.'

The boy went ashen with fear and his bottom lip trembled, but there was a pride and dignity about him worthy of a better fate than the one he was now going to suffer. 'I don't want your religion, priest,' he quavered. He raised his grubby little hand in the communist salute. 'Long live the Red revolution!' he sang out in his high-pitched voice and closed his eyes quickly as the two young troopers aimed.

Du Pres's face flushed angrily. 'Then die, you young Red pig! *Fire*!'

As one the two troopers fired. At that range they couldn't miss. The boy was swept off his feet. He flew through the air and slammed against the nearest wall, his shattered young face sliding down on to his chest like red, molten wax – dead instantly.

Von Dodenburg turned away. He could watch no more.

Ten minutes later they were on their way again, heading south. Behind them as the dark shadows swept down from the mountains across the great river and over the valley floor, the hamlet of Hauterives burned merrily, a funeral pyre to the dead of the *maquis*. Somewhere a lone dog, the sole survivor, howled a mad crazed lament . . .

All that night the long column rolled steadily southwards along the *Route Nationale* Seven under a velvet Midi sky, studded by stars, illuminated by the soft yellow summer moon. Now the trains of wagons and trucks retreating northwards to Lyon were becoming thinner and further apart. They began to encounter more and more men on foot – 'the usual poor shitting stubble-hoppers', as Schulze characterized them. 'They're allus at the frigging sharp end, poor sods!' They didn't look up when the reinforcements rolled by. There were none of the usual contemptuous cries or sarcastic banter that took place when troops were relieved, going in and out of the line. Instead, the infantrymen simply stood there and let the vehicles drive past, numbly, like animals waiting for the slaughter, all passion spent.

Once they passed a group of stragglers, shell-shocked for the most part, von Dodenburg couldn't help thinking, as he saw their pale, fixed, dilated eyes in the warm glow of the moon. They had long ago thrown away their weapons. '*Noi. . .se*,' one said, half whispering, half aloud, moving forward in a daze, '*the noi. . .se . . . noi. . .se . . .*'

Von Dodenburg looked at the soldier as he went by, his pale face vacant, lips trembling.

'Shell-shock,' Schulze said huskily, and added, speaking to no one in particular, 'If we don't snuff it, we all break in the end . . .' The convoy rolled on . . .

By four that morning, they were well south of Valence, rolling down the dead-straight road that led to Montélimar, the panzer grenadiers heaped in the backs of the half-tracks snoring loudly, the gunners and other off-duty men in the tanks and self-propelled guns dozing in their hard seats. Now the countryside seemed empty, as if they were all alone in the world, the last survivors of some nameless catastrophe. Even the stragglers had died away and they had not seen another vehicle driving northwards for over an hour now.

Von Dodenburg's eyes felt as if they were filled with sand and time and time again he fought off the temptation to doze, although, God knows, he was tired enough. But he knew they were approaching a critical phase in their hasty night-march southwards. Montélimar was held; he knew that from the last radio check with the garrison there. But what of the surrounding countryside? Were the *maquis* active there on allied orders? Indeed, what were the Americans themselves doing? Any commander worth his salt would attempt to outflank the place, continue his drive northwards, and let the follow-up infantry mop up Montélimar; or he might simply surround the town with second-line troops and let it wither on the vine.

Sitting there in the jolting cab of the lead half-track, the instruments glowing a bright green in the velvet darkness, a weary, stiff von Dodenburg forced himself to visualize the situation at 'nougat city'. On both sides it was fringed by low mountains, not suitable for tank operations. To the right, as well, the *Route Nationale* Seven was fringed by the River Rhône, crossed by one single bridge, with not another one for twenty kilometres – further north at Loriot. Therefore, he told himself, the right flank could be held easily by, say, a company of infantry and a couple of tanks guarding the bridge across the mighty, fast-flowing Rhône.

He sniffed and watched a shooting star flash across the heavens. He didn't wish. He had long given up any hope that good fortune was on the German side. In this bitter summer of 1944, Germany made its own luck by the courage of its soldiers and force of arms. Instead he addressed himself to the problem of the left flank.

Visualizing the map in his mind's eye, he calculated that he would have a dozen kilometres of open ground to cover with perhaps a thousand men – a very tall order indeed. In fact, it couldn't be done with the resources available to him. He concluded, as they raced ever southwards, that what he *could* do was to deny the road network there to the enemy, so that he couldn't move his armour, forcing him to involve his infantry to capture the roads before the tanks could move. With the aid of the old hares manning the tanks, he could make them pay heavily for each road captured, drawing them ever closer to Montélimar and a fight for a built-up area – and built-up areas could easily swallow up whole divisions of infantry!

'Another Stalingrad?' a cynical little voice sneered inside his head. '"*Stalingrad on the Rhône*" the poison dwarf'll call it . . . But remember this, Kuno. *We Germans lost the Battle of Stalingrad*!'

Kuno von Dodenburg shook his head angrily as if to dismiss that mocking voice. Of course they would lose the Battle of Montélimar. A thousand or more soldiers, however fanatical and brave they were, could not hold up a whole American army indefinitely. But they *could* hold the *Amis* up long enough for Wiese to achieve his aim: the link-up of his 19th Army with the German armies in Normandy.

'And what then, Herr von Dodenburg?' the little voice mocked. 'Where will SS Assault Regiment Wotan be then?'

But Kuno von Dodenburg was unable – or unwilling – to answer that overwhelming question. Slowly he began to drift off into an uneasy sleep . . .

*

He awoke at dawn. Now the convoy was running along the line of the Rhône, the road slightly raised, following the silver snake of the river. The countryside had that chill, early morning, suspended in time, dead atmosphere of ground which had been fought over or would soon be fought over. He sniffed the air and told himself it had the very smell of the front line. How often had he experienced that old smell in these last five years?

Everywhere there were abandoned German vehicles thrust off the road into the ditches on both sides. Here and there the great sheltering trees had been smashed by enemy air attacks, their branches drooping and severed like broken limbs. The road was littered by the blood-red faeces of the retreating army, for now the men of the 19th were suffering from dysentery.

Von Dodenburg rubbed the lines from his face and wished he could wash and shave. But he knew there was no stopping. Soon the enemy *Jabos* would be out looking for new victims. He stretched his stiff limbs and stared at the litter of war flashing by on both sides: rifles, ammunition, belts, grenades, rags of uniform, the crumpled bodies of those grouped around the blackened bomb-craters, everywhere the inevitable paper which seemed to cover every battlefield he had ever seen.

The corporal in charge of the grenadiers passed him a canteen. 'Cold nigger-sweat,* sir,' he announced and winked, 'laced with something a little warmer, though.'

Gratefully von Dodenburg accepted the cold ersatz coffee and took a deep swig. He coughed as the raw brandy slammed into the back of his throat, but he felt new warmth surge through his tired, stiff body and suddenly he was wide awake, his eyes bright and alert, his ears attuned to every new sound. With a hoarse 'thanks' he handed the canteen back to

* Coffee

the corporal and, supporting himself the best he could in the swaying cab, he took his glasses and started to survey the countryside to both sides of the river, as the sun began to ascend, a blood-red ball to the east.

It seemed deserted. Here and there he glimpsed small huddles of white houses with the dark-brown tiles of the roofs almost hidden by cypresses and olive trees. But there was no sign of life in them. No smoke coming from their chimneys, not even the sound of the crowing cocks and gaggling hens. All the same, he had an eerie, creepy feeling that the countryside was not empty; that their progress through this beautiful, bountiful farmland was being watched. Oh yes, there was someone out there all right! The question was who – and what were their intentions?

Schulze, standing high in the turret of the lead Tiger, broad face flushed a blood-red hue in the reflected light of the ascending sun, was preoccupied with the same question. It all looked too easy to his suspicious mind. They had burned down a *maquis* village and slaughtered all its inhabitants, and yet the frog-eaters were doing nothing to gain their revenge, although the field was wide open with the German Army retreating on all sides. It didn't seem right to him.

Down below in the driving compartment, Matz whirled the wheel which adjusted the driver's periscope, blinking suddenly in the bright rays of the rising sun. *There they were*! He wasn't mistaken after all. A small group of horsemen, walking their mounts on the horizon, their outlines a stark black against the crimson ball of the sun. Silent as death at this distance, and somehow very frightening. Ghost riders from another age. With his free hand he pressed his throat-mike and said hoarsely, 'Hey, Schulze, what do yer make o' them fellers with the nags?'

'What fellers with nags, apeturd?' Schulze snapped, irritable as he always was in the early morning.

'Them on the horizon over there – at eight o'clock.'

Schulze swung his head round. The blood-red horizon was empty. 'There's nothing there.'

Matz flung a hasty glance through the periscope. Schulze was right. The riders had vanished into a small cork-wood on the hill. 'But they was there half a mo' ago. I saw them with me own eyes,' he protested.

'Piss in the wind, arse-with-ears!' Schulze barked. 'In this part of the world, they're too poor to have a pot to piss in, never mind gee-gees!'

'But I'm sure, Schulzi,' Matz said fervently. 'I *did* see men with horses. Honest!'

'See the sawbones and get yersen some goggles, old house,' Schulze said easily, stomach rumbling suddenly as he visualized a great coil of greasy salami washed down with steaming hot coffee and a shot of schnapps for breakfast. He smacked his cracked lips, as if in anticipation. 'You're seeing things, mate, cos you ain't had nothing to eat for the last twelve hours. The sawbones call it hallu . . . well, yer seeing things, take it from me.'

'Are you sure, Schulzi?' Matz asked uncertainly, staring at the horizon, which remained stubbornly empty.

'Of course, I'm sure . . . It's all a frigging figleaf of yer frigging imagination, take it from Papa Schulze. Now you settle down and keep yer mind on the road, or else Papa Schulze'll have to send for the gents in the white coats to take yer away in their rubber van . . .'

Matz relapsed into a moody silence and concentrated on the road, though he kept looking to the glowing horizon. But it was always empty. In the end he gave up, telling himself Schulze was right. It had all been a figleaf of his frigging imagination!

CHAPTER 5

They rode easily, the thick white dust of the country road, that wound between the vines, muffling the sound of their horses' hooves, field-grey tunics open at the neck, savouring the faint breeze coming from the Rhône. Now they could hear the roar of the convoy's motors quite clearly, although they themselves were well hidden on the sunken road that led to the *Route Nationale*. Up front, Bogdan crossed himself in the elaborate Ukrainian fashion, knowing that soon it would happen and that many of them would die in this desperate mission that the *maquis* had forced upon them. But then, he told himself, they would die anyway, more than likely. They had betrayed Russia in order to fight for Germany, hoping that by fighting for the *nmetski*, they might achieve the freedom of their oppressed homeland from Moscow. Now that the Germans were virtually defeated here in France and they had turned to the Resistance for succour, they found themselves being forced to fight against their former masters. Bogdan tugged at the reins of his sweat-sleek mount and told himself it was a crazy world.

Their pace slackened. They started to climb a slight hill that overlooked the main road. The dust rose about their mounts' bellies. Now Bogdan in the lead could hear the noise of the long column quite distinctly, as the drivers changed down furiously to take the bend and the steep gradient beyond. Carefully Bogdan dismounted and handed the reins of his horse to his servant. Behind him the riders came to a halt, already unslinging their carbines. Bogdan nodded his approval, his swarthy face beneath the rakishly tilted fur cap, still bearing the eagle badge of the *Wehrmacht*, suddenly set. Soon it would happen - and there'd be casualties. Pulling out his pistol, he stole forward alone.

He breasted the rise carefully, body hunched low, and

stopped. As the Resistance men had told him, here the steep incline and the bend would separate some of the vehicles from the main convoy. While a half a dozen half-tracks ground their way up the height in first gear, perhaps another dozen or so were working around the corner laboriously, their sweating, cursing drivers clashing through their gears furiously. Beyond, another ten lorries slowed down and waited their turn. Bogdan stroked his long straggling moustache thoughtfully. All the Resistance had asked of him was that he slowed the convoy down. Why, he did not know or care. All he was concerned with was that the Resistance officially accepted his cavalry into their movement; that would remove the stigma of having fought for the Germans from them. Then, after the battle of southern France was over, he and his men would quietly do a dive. There were plenty of émigré organisations he knew of in Paris that would help them. God willing, they might even be able to continue the fight to free their homeland from communist tyranny from there. But, first, they had to prove themselves to the Resistance. 'Stop the boche for two hours,' they had promised him when he had first approached them after they had deserted from the 19th Army, 'and you are free men, members of the *maquis*, part of the Allied cause.'

Bogdan frowned and took another long look at the terrain, running an expert eye across it. As a young man he had fought for the Ukrainian Liberation Army; later he had been conscripted into the Red Army. After that had come the *Wehrmacht*; now he was fighting for the French, it seemed. And always he had survived because he had paid a great deal of attention to the ground over which he was going to fight.

Here, there were advantages, but also problems. Undoubtedly he would catch the dozen or so soft-skinned vehicles down there, waiting to ascend the hill by surprise. But beyond there were at least five hundred metres of open country before they could reach the cover of the small wood beyond. A good steady German gunner, armed with a high velocity machine-gun, could cause heavy casualties among his cavalry before they could do that. What was the answer? It came to him almost instantly. Not a hit-and-run raid as was the custom of cavalry on the attack, but the one hundred percent slaughter of the *nmetski* so that there would be no good steady German gunners left to mow them down as they fled. Bogdan's swarthy, pock-marked face cracked into a knowing smile. '*Da, da*,' he said softly to himself, 'that is it . . . *There will have to be a massacre* . . .' Swiftly he turned and made his way back to his horse.

The whore Lisa was happy. The squad of *Milice* men she had quickly serviced before the convoy had set off had been very appreciative. Now she munched the chocolates they had given her and sipped the sweet champagne straight from the bottle, enjoying the kind of breakfast she had only dreamt about for years. Admittedly it had been hard work tackling ten randy French police in a hurry behind the truck, but it had been worth it. She shivered with delight and bit into soft-centred chocolate.

Opposite her Rosi-Rosi, named after her enormous bright red nipples, the size of two overripe plums, was idly brushing her pubic hair with one hand and reading the magazine spread out across her ample lap with the other. 'After all, a girl has always to be prepared, specially in wartime. The customers like to see a well-brushed, powdered split-beaver,' she had announced sweetly earlier on.

Now as the truck driven by one of the *Milice* slowed down prior to taking the height, she said to no one in particular, for most of the whores were still trying to wake up after a long boring night's journey, 'Look at it!' She slapped the pornographic magazine with a plump, beringed hand. 'The usual stuff. Two dames doing it to one another, looking as bored as hell.' She sighed. 'I can never figure men being interested in that kind of thing. After all, lezzies are not interested in men, are they?'

Lisa swallowed yet another chocolate and said, 'There's no

accounting for men's tastes, dearie. I once knew a feller who had to stick an ice cube up his arse before –' She stopped suddenly, chocolate in an abruptly open mouth half eaten.

'What is it, Lisa?' Rosi-Rosi asked urgently, the two women with cropped hair doing something impossible to each other immediately forgotten.

'What's that noise outside? Sounds like horses or something.' Lisa frowned and hastily swallowed the chocolate, grabbing for another at the same time, as if someone might well steal it from beneath her big nose. 'Have a look out of the back.'

Modestly pressing a plump arm across her enormous breasts to conceal them from any prying soldier's eyes and not doing a very good job of it, which was not surprising with the amount of naked flesh she had to cover, Rosi-Rosi opened the flap at the back of the truck. She gasped with shock.

'What is it?' Lisa cried, noting the ashen look on her friend's face.

'*Horsemen . . . Look*!' Rosi-Rosi thrust the canvas further aside and now it was Lisa's turn to gasp as she saw the riders racing towards them, bent low over the necks of their flying steeds, their sabres flashing silver in the light of the rising sun, with already to their rear, the first wild burst of machine-gun fire from the startled *Milice*. She shuddered with fear. 'We're in trouble,' she quavered and grabbed for her blouse.

Rosi-Rosi, the supreme realist, not taking her eyes off the charging cavalry, sneered, 'Trouble we are in, Lisa, and it's no frigging use putting on yer clothes, for them friggers are just gonna tear 'em off'n yer agen . . . *Here they frigging well come* . . !'

'*Abandon them*!' Marchant snapped, face set and hard, as he, du Pres and von Dodenburg stared at the message the sweating radio operator had just handed them.

'*But they are your Milice for the most part*!' von Dodenburg objected fervently, his ears taking in the muted snap-and-crackle of small-arms fire now.

'They knew that they would be expected to pay the butcher's bill one day when they first joined the *Milice*,' Marchant answered coldly. 'They will fight bravely and to the end, knowing there is no hope for them.'

'*Mais, mon fils* –' du Pres began, but Marchant stopped him short.

'Don't give me any of that "my son" crap!' he snorted. 'God is not going to help us Frenchmen this summer. It's already too late for God.' His dark burning face was cast for a moment in a sneer of absolute contempt. 'We have to help ourselves. Our mission is to reach Montélimar as soon as possible and take over the defence. The fate of a score or so policemen is of no importance in that light.' He snapped his fingers angrily as if dismissing the matter.

'But they are your men – *Frenchmen*!' du Pres persisted. 'You can't just abandon them like that.'

'All this war, the French have lived a good life,' Marchant answered coldly. 'They've stuffed their guts, had their whores, made good money in the war factories, put plenty of dough away in their stockings, while the rest of Europe has suffered. Let them learn now what war and hardship is about . . .' He turned away moodily and lit one of his cheap cigars.

Du Pres looked at the tall SS officer a little helplessly, while the latter considered. He knew the importance of reaching Montélimar; at the same time it went against the grain to abandon one's own men, even if they were Frenchmen. The code of the SS maintained one should be prepared to sacrifice one's own life for a comrade. *What the devil was he going to do*?

Next to him, du Pres bowed his head and was beginning to pray, a strange sound in that place, with the angry rattle of machine-guns and the dry crack of riflefire becoming ever louder: '*Oh God, look down in mercy on us all this dawn, friend and foe . . . Let Thy fatherly hand guide those who make decisions, succour the wounded, strengthen the dying . . .*'

But it was neither the code of the SS nor du Pres's appeal to God which finally made up von Dodenburg's mind for him. It was Schulze's rough awkward, 'Sir, you know that them whores I . . . er . . . rescued are down there, don't you, sir . . . I mean they might be whores,' he tugged the end of his big sunburnt nose, as if suddenly embarrassed, 'but they're women, too, *German* women, and we all know what the frog-eaters'll do to them if they get captured . . .' He stopped short and looked down at his big dusty boots.

Von Dodenburg made up his mind. Almost angrily he snapped to the praying priest, 'Major du Pres, form an immediate attack-group for an attack to the rear . . . You, Schulze, you will lead a section of three tanks to support them. And for God's sake watch those ditches. I need those Tigers like I need my arm. Don't you dare lose a single one of them . . .'

Five minutes later they were on their way, du Pres's troopers clinging tightly to the rear of the big tanks as they started to roll down the hill towards the site of the massacre, while von Dodenburg stared miserably at the bright blue wash of the dawn sky wondering when exactly the *Jabos* would hit his stalled convoy . . .

CHAPTER 6

Bogdan tugged savagely at the bit. His horse whinnied with pain and reared up on its hind legs. On all sides there were the gruff cries and drunken shouts of his men, intermingled with the odd shot, as they looted the French trucks. As always on such occasions, his cavalry had got out of hand. Just like their half-wild, savage ancestors before them, they threw all discipline and order to the winds at the prospect of loot and women; for he could hear the shrill, hysterical screams of women coming from higher up the road. He spurred his horse forward through the drunken, wolfish throng, slashing to left and right with his reins, trying to beat some sense into his men before it was too late. 'Come on, *davai . . . davai*,' he cried. 'Leave it! We must be on our way at once . . . *Davai . . . davai*!'

He reached out and slashed savagely at a soldier rifling through a suitcase, carelessly tossing clothes and papers over his shoulder as he sought valuables. 'Come on, you big fool!' he roared. 'Time is running out!'

But this dramatic dawn his men weren't listening to Bogdan. Their lives were short and brutish; they took their pleasures as they came, even if they did die doing so.

He came upon half a dozen drunken cavalrymen attempting to rip the clothes off a screaming fat blonde, her great dangling dugs hanging over a yellow belly scarred with old operations. On the road next to her, next to the body of a *Milice*, his throat slit raggedly from ear to ear, another of his men, pants ripped down to his boots, was savagely humping another screaming, writhing German woman with nipples like bright red plums; while a drunken comrade patted him enthusiastically on his hectically heaving buttocks, crying, 'Ride her, Sasha . . . Ride her for the Motherland, you whore-jockey!' He laughed uproariously at his own humour and passed out.

Bogdan grabbed for his pistol. He had to stop the rot before it was too late. Already he could hear the sinister rumble and squeak of heavy tanks above him on the heights, and a faint droning in the sky which he could not quite identify. He snapped off the safety and aimed. The cavalryman humping Rosi-Rosi screamed shrilly. A sudden dark-red flush covered the skin of his back. His spine arched impossibly. Suddenly jetting bright-scarlet blood, he fell dead on Rosi-Rosi, who had been killed by the same bullet. Bogdan raised his pistol and fired the rest of the magazine into the sky.

The slugs had their effect. Abruptly the drunken cavalrymen froze where they stood, faces ashen and shocked, suddenly sober, like actors at the final curtain of some third-rate melodrama. Bogdan, his face flushed brick-red with anger, leaned forward, pistol raised, and lashed the muzzle back and forth against the face of the nearest soldier. 'You swine, you stupid swine!' he cried beside himself with rage, 'do you want to get us all killed, son of a whore . . ! Can't you hear them coming? *Yo tuoya mat*!' He shrieked that coarse soldiers' oath as the soldier reeled back, face a bloody mess, black blood trickling from his shattered nostrils. 'On your feet. *The Tigers are coming*!'

In a flash the cavalrymen realized the danger they were in. All of them knew there was nothing that could stop that sixty-ton monster. In Normandy a mere handful of them had wiped out a whole British brigade of tanks and infantry, three thousand men strong. They had no wish to be similarly massacred. Suddenly the women and the loot were forgotten. In an instant they were running furiously for their mounts, while that curious drone grew louder and louder . . .

'Left . . . *a little more left, fuck you*!' Schulze cried urgently, as a sweating Matz down below in the driver's compartment edged the big tank millimetre by millimetre around the steep bend which led to the descent. Behind them the other Tigers ground to a halt, du Pres's SS men crouching behind their massive bulks carefully, for their still unknown attackers were not far off now.

Cursing furiously Matz fought the tank round the bend, the broad tracks racing, coming perilously close to the edge of the drop below. It had been bad enough getting the sixty-ton tank up the height; it was worse taking it down. One false move and it might well slide right over.

But even as a harassed Schulze guided his old running-mate down the treacherous descent, his ears were already attuned to the roar of the planes coming from the south. Without even having to look up, he knew who they would be – *the Americans*! These days the *Luftwaffe* had virtually disappeared from the skies of France. They would never make an appearance in such numbers as that heavy ominous drone suggested.

For a moment he simply stood there in the turret, bemused by that awesome spectacle of over one hundred bombers heading straight for him; then it came to him with the total immediacy of a revelation. There might be a way to fool the bastards after all!

Often they had bombed their own troops rather than come low enough to identify them accurately; and their own ground-troops knew it. They were always exceedingly careful to identify their own positions exactly.

'Gunner,' he barked, 'unload HE at once.'*

'Sir,' the young gunner snapped and jerked back the breech-handle. Next to him the loader hauled out the great gleaming brass shell-case hurriedly.

'Load green marker-smoke,' Schulze ordered, mind racing desperately. 'Plant one to left and right of those trucks down there.' He indicated the stalled vehicles with the cavalry milling around them in a flurry of dust.

'Sir!'

Schulze didn't wait for the gunner to open fire. Instead, he pressed his throat-mike hastily and cried, 'Identification

* High Explosive

arrows out – at the double . . . Point them towards the road below . . . Don't ask frigging questions . . . Just do as I say. Move it now. Get yer party frocks on, lads, we're going to the ball –'

The rest of his words were drowned by the crack and thunder of the big gun as the first smoke-shell started to wing its way towards the cavalry.

As the shell exploded a hundred metres away in the vineyard to his right, and thick bright-green smoke began to billow up from it almost immediately, Bogdan knew that the tables had been turned. The Resistance had wanted him to hold up the German convoy until those sinister silver bombers up there arrived to carry out their deadly work. They hadn't cared one hoot whether his men were killed in the bombing raid or not. They were simply expendable cannonfodder. Now the Germans on the heights were trying to trick the Americans into bombing them. Already he could see the red flares sailing into the air over the German positions to indicate to the American pilots that it would be dangerous to drop their bombs there, for they were friendly positions.

Another shell shrieked in and exploded to the left, neatly bracketing the confused cavalry, and instantly another pillar of green smoke began streaming upwards. '*Boshe moi*!' Bogdan cursed and dug the bit into his horse's mouth savagely. It reared up and round. '*Davai . . . davai . . . Hurry, scatter, men, for God's sake . . . before it's too late* –'

But it was already too late. The whine of the first bombs turned into a furious series of explosions. The earth erupted in one colossal heave. Bogdan screamed, high, shrill and hysterical like a woman, as the earth quivered and trembled beneath him in elemental fury. The hard silver slivers of metal flying everywhere ripped and tore at his mount. It went down in a mass of flailing legs, whinnying piteously, its stomach ripped out, its life-blood jetting from it.

Bogdan scrambled to his feet. There was no time now to

draw his pistol and end the poor creature's sufferings. Riders and horses were going down everywhere, piling up in a chaotic confused mass of dying men and animals. Steel hissed through the air like heavy tropical rain. Man after man went down. Riderless horses, terrified out of their minds, galloped off across the cratered fields, rearing and plunging, snorting with wide-nostrilled, unreasoning fear. And still those cruel bombs came whistling down.

With the rest Bogdan blundered frantically through the vineyard, gasping crazily for breath, seized by the same unreasoning fear as the rest, leaving the wounded to care for themselves, deaf to their terrified pleas for help and the pitiful whinnying of the dying horses.

And then they were gone. They had played their part in the history of World War Two – a mere scratch on the long wall of history – victims from the day they were born to the day they were to die in violent obscurity . . .

Schulze watched, as the silver bombers now began to turn, their mission of death completed now, sailing round at twenty thousand feet, leaving their brilliant white contrails behind them, and spat drily. He took no pleasure in that scene of death before him: the slaughtered horses and their dead riders scattered everywhere like bundles of abandoned rags; the raped, naked whores, their blood-stained thighs spread in obscene invitation; the *Milice*, their throats cut savagely, their genitals severed as was the custom; death and destruction as far as the eye could see.

'Frigging flyboys,' he snorted morosely. 'Look at 'em! They've slaughtered a couple of hundred poor sods from up there, a kilometre or more up in the sky, and they don't even know they've frigging well done it! Now they're off home back to mother to frigging bacon and eggs and bed with some fat whore to keep 'em warm.' He spat again. '*Frigging flyboys*!'

Further up the column, Colonel von Dodenburg's thoughts were just as sombre, as the first salvo burst at the edge of the road, sending up clods of the rich red earth and fragments of suddenly charred wood spinning and flying. Seconds later, further shell-bursts erupted on the other side of the road, sending the tankers ducking and running for cover.

Von Dodenburg remained upright in the turret, sweeping the area with his binoculars. 'They're bracketing us,' he announced to Lieutenant Krings. He ducked automatically, as a shower of small stones rattled against the side of the turret and the young lieutenant wondered at the CO's calm. They had escaped a horrendous bombing attack; now they were being attacked from the land. Yet Colonel von Dodenburg remained absolutely cool, almost as if the whole deadly business bored him.

'There they are!' Von Dodenburg cut into his reverie. 'Over there on the right flank at four o'clock.'

Krings raised his glasses hastily and focused them. Small squat objects, which he recognized immediately, slid into the gleaming calibrated circles of glass noisily. 'Shermans,' he said. 'Aren't they, sir?'

Von Dodenburg nodded, not lowering his glasses, watching the American tanks scuttle in and out of the trees a kilometre or so away, pausing only to fire and then hurrying off again. Finally he did so and said slowly, as if it was a matter of little importance, 'Shermans they are, Krings.' He sighed. 'So one thing is clear. The *Amis* have outflanked Montélimar. They've won that part of the race.' He paused and stroked his unshaven chin.

Krings waited and then when the CO did not speak, seemingly oblivious to the enemy shell-fire, he blurted out, 'And what does that mean, sir . . . For us, I mean?'

'What does it mean?' von Dodenburg echoed. He laughed grimly. 'It means, my dear Lieutenant Krings, that when we advance now, we will be putting our heads into a sack. And now that the *Amis* are on our flanks, yes, there are more Shermans over there to the left, they can pull the neck of that sack closed at any time that suits them.'

Krings gasped, as the full importance of what the CO had

just said overcame him. 'You mean, sir,' he stuttered, as the shell-fire grew ever closer, 'that the *Amis* will be able to cut us off from the rear? We'll be isolated . . . in Montélimar?' He stared wild-eyed at von Dodenburg, a nerve at the side of his temple suddenly beginning to tick.

'Exactly. As that rogue Sergeant Schulze would put it in his own inimitable fashion, soon SS Assault Regiment Wotan is going to be right up to its hooter in shit once again . . . All right, let's not hang around here any more. Let's get our party frocks and get ready for the dance.' He smiled cynically at the perplexed younger officer and waved his right hand. 'Roll 'em,' he yelled. '*Roll 'em, everybody*!'

Slowly the column got underway again, heading south to the beleagured French city and Wotan's date with destiny this bloody August in the year 1944 . . .

BOOK THREE

The Battle of Nougat City

CHAPTER 1

Panic reigned.

As the first of Wotan's vehicles began to roll into the French town, the shells already falling on its centre, von Dodenburg could see that the rot had already set in. There were scruffy infantrymen wandering around without weapons, their hands in their pockets, eyes frightened and furtive. Gunners had abandoned their anti-tank guns dug into each side of the road heading north, and were lounging in doorways, faces apprehensive. Somewhere in a side-street there was the sound of breaking glass and drunken singing; obviously the defenders were already beginning to loot the place. And the long stream of shabbily dressed refugees, their pathetic bits and pieces piled up on carts, heading north out of the town, was a sure sign that they knew what was to come. They were getting out of Montélimar while the going was good.

'*Canaille*!' Marchant, standing next to von Dodenburg in the turret of the Tiger, rolled his cigar to the corner of his mouth and spat contemptuously. 'How brave we French are! The first sign of trouble and we fill our breeches!'

Von Dodenburg frowned. He didn't care about the fleeing civilians; they were fewer mouths to feed in the siege to come. But he was concerned about the soldiers lounging about everywhere. The first sight of an enemy Sherman and they'd run; fear was written on all their unshaven faces. He opened his mouth to comment but the enemy *Jabo* beat him to it.

Without warning, its approach drowned by the rumble of gunfire, the Thunderbolt fell from the sky, vicious red and white tracer spitting from its stubby wings. The infantry yelled and bellowed in panic, scattering wildly, those still armed throwing away their weapons in their haste to find cover. Next moment the Thunderbolt was flashing - a bright silver - into the burning blue sky once more, twisting and turning exuberantly at the success of its sudden strike; then it vanished. But von Dodenburg knew there would be more. The American vice around Montélimar was beginning to tighten.

Now the infantry began to stream out of their hiding places again. But they did not pick up their weapons. Instead they stood around in morose groups, chatting softly, throwing furtive glances at the long column of SS men, obviously waiting for them to be gone so that they could desert.

Von Dodenburg made it a sudden decision. 'Stop the tank!' he cried and below, Matz braked immediately. Hardly waiting for the Tiger to stop, von Dodenburg dropped over the side to the littered cobbles. Schulze followed, holding his machine-pistol in his hands at the ready, glaring fiercely at the shame-faced shabby infantrymen.

Angrily von Dodenburg strode over to the nearest group. 'You!' he barked to a fat, bespectacled corporal who dangled a cigarette from his slack wet lips, 'Come here . . . *at the double now*!'

Hesitantly, he came forward and clicked to attention, his face fearful yet defiant.

'Where's your personal weapon, Corporal?' von Dodenburg barked, looking him up and down, every inch a typical arrogant SS officer, ignoring the angry murmuring coming from the rest of the watching infantry. 'And take that damned lung-torpedo out of your mouth when you're speaking to an officer!' Von Dodenburg didn't wait for the fat corporal to comply. Instead he slapped his hand savagely across the man's mouth, knocking the cigarette from his slack lips. It was a calculated act of brutality, aimed at intimidating the waverers.

The corporal's eyes flushed with tears. 'You ain't got the right to do that, even if you are an officer!' he stuttered. 'Officers ain't allowed to strike private soldiers.'

Behind von Dodenburg, Schulze clicked off his safety significantly and the corporal blanched. He swayed, as if he might well faint.

'Listen you fat sack,' von Dodenburg snapped, 'I can do exactly what I want and this is my authority.' He slapped his pistol holster and the corporal jumped, startled. 'Now get your weapon and get a grip of your men. The *Amis* are just up that road behind and they'll be coming soon. And I warn you, if you desert your post again,' von Dodenburg's icy-blue eyes bored into the corporal's fat, frightened face, 'it won't be a slap across your blubbery chops; you'll get a merry little jig – *at the end of a rope*! *Now move it*!'

The fat corporal 'moved it'.

But as the column pushed deeper into the French town, von Dodenburg could see that things were in a bad way. From the plane trees which sheltered the street from the summer heat there were men in field-grey hanging, their tongues protruding from purple lips, eyes bulging from their sockets, their breeches wet where they had evacuated their bladders with the intense pain. Each one bore a rough and ready placard hanging from his neck, reading: '*I was a defeatist and a coward. I have suffered a just fate. Let this be a warning to all defeatists and cowards.*'

Marchant nodded his head in approval. 'I see the Gestapo have been at work,' he observed. 'That's the only way to put backbone into the cowardly swine.'

For his part, von Dodenberg remained silent, face set and grim. How in three devils' name was he going to defend this city with a thousand odd men and this bunch of stubble-hoppers who would obviously break and make a run for it once the balloon went up? *How*?

'*How*?' Police-General Hartmann hissed in that eerie lisp of his, stroking his lobster-pink nose as if to reassure himself that the plastic surgeon's work was still in place. 'Terror, my dear Colonel, that's the answer. They've got to be more afraid of General Hartmann that they will be of the *Amis*.' He attempted to smile, but the glass eye remained set in a stiff unwinking stare in the livid pink hole which was all that remained of the left side of his face. Once he had been a fine, handsome figure of a man. Now he was a crippled monster, his face an atrocity which the finest of the Third Reich's plastic surgeons had been unable to rectify, one arm hanging down his side like a withered black talon. Even du Pres, standing stiffly to attention at von Dodenberg's side, was visibly awed by the general's monstrous injuries.

Hartmann caught their looks and said sternly through his great yellow false teeth set against the bright pink plastic gums, again the work of the plastic surgeon. '*Einsatzgruppe** in east Poland, Forty-three. Surprised by a bunch of damned Polack partisans. We beat them off in the end, of course. But they did this to me. Grenade in the old mug. Not very pretty, what? Even my lady wife has screaming fits when every now and again I have occasion to remind her of my marital rights. . . . These days, alas, the Hartmanns rarely dance that delightful mattress polka together.'

Von Dodenberg forced a grin. Monster he might be, this police general in charge of Montélimar, but he did have a bitter sense of humour; and with the defences of the city falling apart all around him, he would undoubtedly need that humour.

'So,' Hartmann continued, 'with the gentlemen of the Gestapo who have not yet fled, I have . . . er . . . *encouraged* my brave soldiers to believe that there is still a need for them to fight and, if necessary, die for Folk, Fatherland, and Führer.'

Marchant's dark eyes blazed, as did those of du Pres. Spontaneously, the two of them flung up their right hands and cried fervently, '*Sieg Heil*!'

Casually Hartmann flipped up his good hand and hissed in a bored cynical way, 'Oh, yes. *Sieg Heil*!'

Von Dodenburg grinned again. Not only did the general have a sense of humour, he was apparently a cynic, too. Obviously he did not rate National Socialist patriotism very highly any more.

* Nazi extermination squads used in the East against Jews and partisans

'What have you got in the way of bodies, sir?' von Dodenburg asked. 'And what do you know of the movements of the enemy?'

Hartmann turned to him. 'Bodies is the operative word, *Obersturmbannführer*. Two thousand, roughly. They will do to take the first brunt of the enemy attack. When they've all gone hop, as you front swine put it, then it'll be up to you fellers of the SS, and naturally,' he turned his monstrous cynical gaze on to the two French officers, 'our brave allies. The enemy? What do I know about them?' He crooked a finger at the three officers. 'Let me *show* you the enemy.'

In a heavy silence, broken only by the rumble of the American guns and the snarl of the diving *Jabos*, the four of them stared out of the window of the tall villa which housed Hartmann's headquarters. '*Voila*, gentlemen, there is the enemy!'

Even von Dodenburg could not quite repress a gasp of surprise. About a kilometre and a half away, where the town ended and the vineyards of the area began, there were tiny hulks of Shermans everywhere, scuttling in and out of the farms, while, to their front, lines of infantry moved across the fields in slow, silent concentration like countrymen plodding home after a hard day's work on the land. On all sides there were gun batteries busily digging in, with jeeps and ambulances careering back and forth in clouds of white dust, while above them the spotter planes and the fighters roared about their missions. To von Dodenburg it was as if he were viewing some sand-table model back at officers' school, only with one difference: the weapons and men out there weren't models. They really fired – *and killed*!

'*Himmelherrgott*, General,' he cursed, surprised at the enemy's strength. 'There must be at least a division out there!'

'A division and a half, to be exact, *Obersturmbannführer*, according to my intelligence,' Hartmann said calmly.

Von Dodenburg's brain raced as he tried to work out the odds, but Hartmann, the cynic, beat him to it. 'Yes, my dear von Dodenburg, some twenty thousand first class American troops, bountifully supplied with armour and aircraft and all those other mechanical goodies that Uncle Sugar produces, against two thousand, hm, what shall we say?' He gave von Dodenburg that horrible lopsided smile of his, '*Bodies*, plus one thousand of your people, French and German. The odds are decidedly in the enemy's favour, one might say.'

Von Dodenburg nodded his head sombrely and Marchant glared fiercely at the American lines, while du Pres, the ex-priest, lowered his head as if he might well be saying a quick prayer for divine intervention.

Suddenly there was iron in Hartmann's voice and the cynicism had gone. 'All the same, we will stop them. Big and well-fed as they are, they think they can stand off and let their mechanical toys do all their dirty work for them. Well, they are mistaken.' Hartmann's one eye blazed fire. 'Outnumbered as we are, gentlemen, we will stop them here in Montélimar. If there is going to have to be another Stalingrad in France, let it be here, at Montélimar! *Nougat* is this place's claim to fame – up to now. Let us give it a more honourable place in history. Let Montélimar be the town where a handful of brave men and a heap of trash stopped the might of the American Army!'

Almost as if to emphasize that moment of high drama, a great shell slammed into the building opposite, and it disappeared in a great angry burst of bright-red flame. The God of War had spoken. The Battle of 'Nougat City' could commence . . .

CHAPTER 2

Now the dive-bombers were departing. As the smoke-columns, flecked a cherry-red here and there with the fires, started to ascend slowly into the leaden sky, the Thunderbolts and the Lightnings soared high into the air, followed by the lethal morse of the flak and anti-aircraft machine-guns. The sirens commenced sounding the all-clear.

Everywhere the soldiers and the civilians emerged from the cellars and bunkers to find a transformed Montélimar: a stark macabre horror. Whole blocks of workers' houses had been wiped out, transformed into a steaming, crazy landscape of twisted girders, dangling beams, shattered masonry. The trees which had lined the streets had snapped off like giant matchsticks. Everywhere there were smoking bomb craters in the streets like the work of monstrous moles. But it was not the shattered buildings which caught the attention of the Wotan troopers as they emerged from their dugouts on the southernmost edge of the city. It was the piles of dead stacked up on all sides like heaps of cordwood, civilians and soldiers sprawled together, clutching each other in the violence of sudden death, like lovers in a passionate embrace.

'Holy strawsack!' Schulze gasped, as now the American guns took up the battle once more, following the dive-bombing attack. 'It's worse than Hamburg in Forty-three.' He tried not to see the naked baby, its clothes ripped off by the blast, impaled on an iron railing across the way like some sort of monstrous toffee-apple. 'Christ, what murdering pigs those Americans are! Can't they fight fair?'

Matz laughed drily. 'What kind of horseshit is that?' he grunted. '*Fighting fair*! Wars are never frigging fair –' He grabbed Schulze's arm hurriedly, alarmed by the short thundering roar, and pulled him to one side. Just in time. The wall directly in front of them came crumbling and hissing down to crash to the ground in a cloud of thick white choking dust, sending the two of them off coughing like ancient asthmatics in the throes of a fatal attack.

'*Shit, shit, shit* . . . !' Schulze gasped and choked, spitting out the dust. 'Is there going to be no frigging peace for the frigging wicked?'

'No,' a well-known voice snapped nearby. 'Well, not for you at least.' Schulze staggered round, still gasping. It was the CO, Colonel von Dodenburg, his face set and grim, and very businesslike, under his dust-covered steel helmet. Schulze made an attempt to come to attention, but von Dodenburg waved for him to desist, muttering, 'No time for playing soldiers now, you big rogue. I've got a mission for you and the other Tiger crews.'

'Mission?' the two of them echoed in unison, as the big 155mm shells ripped the heavens apart and once again began falling on the centre of the besieged city.

'But, sir,' Schulze protested, 'I've been in the line all night as infantry. I thought I might cock my leg over –'

'You'll cock your leg over the turret of your Tiger!' von Dodenburg interrupted him brutally. 'That's the only kind of evil fornication you will be doing this day, Schulze.'

Schulze looked duly glum and von Dodenburg said, 'Now don't worry. I don't think we're going to have our pinkies slapped this day somehow. So far, as you know, the *Amis* have had it their own way. They've been bombing and shelling us for twelve hours now, obviously softening us up for an all-out attack.' He ducked as another great shell whistled out of the sky and thumped to the ground with an earth-shaking roar a couple of hundred metres away. 'Now, General Hartmann and I think they ought to have a couple of their teeth drawn smartly. Might just put them off their stride, especially as they seem to think we are not capable of offensive action.'

'How do you mean, sir?' Matz asked.

'Well, like this.' With the toe of his boot von Dodenburg drew a line in the dust. 'This is the main railway line from Lyon to Marseille, with the railway embankment running alongside it. Got it?' The two of them nodded. 'Well on the left side of the embankment, which is a good three metres high, there is a dug-in anti-tank gun and some infantry, perhaps a couple of platoons at the most. And on the other side of that embankment is the mass of their Shermans, preparing for the armoured thrust, once their infantry attack. Now, say, Major Marchant's *Milice* took out those infantrymen and the anti-tank gun, there would be no stopping –'

'Our Tigers from rolling up that embankment, concealed from the Shermans on the other side, and sticking our salamis right up the *Ami* Shermans!' Matz broke in excitedly.

'Exactly,' von Dodenburg said. 'Of course, there's some risk involved, but it might well put the *Amis* off their stroke. They are a methodical people. Once a plan has broken down, it takes them some considerable time to re-group and begin all over again.' Von Dodenburg paused and mopped his sweat-glazed brow. 'Besides, any small kind of victory we can achieve over the Americans will be good for the morale of the garrison.' He looked worried suddenly. 'And they certainly need some stiffening.'

If von Dodenburg was worried about the outcome of the surprise attack, Schulze wasn't. He raised his heavy right haunch, cracked off an enormous fart, and cried exuberantly, '*Arseholes up*! *Three cheers for America*!'

Von Dodenburg smiled wearily and told himself that if someone could only give him a thousand Schulzes, he'd beat the whole goddam world!

'*There was an old man of Graz, who swallowed a blade of Grass*,' Schulze sung softly to himself, as the column of Tigers swung past the dead anti-tank gunners, Marchant's cops busy looting the bodies for cigarettes and money. '*One grew from his earhole and the other grew straight out of his arse . . .*'

Now they were running through rough, undulating countryside, their right flank well protected by the high overgrown embankment from the unsuspecting Americans on the other side of it. Now the landscape seemed to von Dodenburg to have that tense, empty look that always seemed to signify a coming battlefield. It was as though the very earth were dreading the slaughter to come.

Von Dodenburg shook himself out of his reverie and concentrated on the task ahead. 'Matz,' he snapped through the mike, 'swing into that next cutting. Two and three follow . . . Krings.'

'Sir?'

'You take the remaining three and go through the next cutting up there . . . a hundred metres on. We'll rendezvous on the other side. And take it easy, Krings. *Hals und Beinbruch*!'

'Thank you, sir.'

'Over and out!' von Dodenburg said hurriedly, as carefully Matz swung the huge tank into the dank, dripping cutting through the embankment. He strained his eyes in the sudden darkness. Yes, there they were, the unsuspecting American Shermans, their crews sprawled on their decks, smoking and chatting, with others crouched on their haunches over little flickering blue fires, obviously cooking their rations. There was even a small group of them stripped to their shorts, sun-glasses on, skinny bodies gleaming with suntan oil.

'Holy Moses!' Schulze gasped with shock. 'Did you ever see the like of it, sir? Sun-bathing in the middle of a frigging war! Wow, all Americans must be crazy!'

Von Dodenburg didn't reply. He was concentrating on getting his six Tigers through the cuttings and into action before the Americans woke up to their danger.

Now all six Tigers were out in the open, nosing their way cautiously through the vines heavy with unpicked grapes, their advance still unnoticed by the American tankers lolling in the sun. Von Dodenburg licked his lips time and time again, assailed by that tense expectancy of impending battle, his nerve-ends tingling, his vision acutely clear as he swept the lines of Shermans waiting for the first panic. How casual and at ease these Americans seemed, as if the war were a thousand kilometres away, full of that naïve transatlantic confidence of theirs that *nothing* could happen to the fortunate sons of Uncle Sam. Grimly, he told himself that a goodly number of Uncle Sam's sons would not survive to see the end of this burningly hot summer's day.

'Six hundred metres, sir!' Schulze's voice cut into his thoughts, peering through the big gun's telescope.

'Stand by,' von Dodenburg said, pressing his throat-mike, noting with surprise just how calm and routine his own voice sounded.

His crews repeated the order one by one. 'Five hundred and fifty!' Schulze said.

'Driver reduce speed . . . commanders pick individual targets,' von Dodenburg commanded, as Matz below crashed through a dozen gears to reduce the sixty-ton monster's speed.

Schulze pressed his cruelly muscled shoulder against the leather pad of the gun. His hand sought and found the trigger handle. Squinting a little, trying to control his breathing, he centred the crosswires of the sight on a Sherman, complete with sun-bathing crew. He started to count off the seconds. It wouldn't be long now. Everywhere the huge tanks, against which the Shermans were virtually powerless, under-gunned and under-armoured as they were, went into the hull down position.

Von Dodenburg flashed a look to right and left. Every gun was now trained on the still unsuspecting Americans lolling in the sun. He opened his mouth to give the order to fire. But that wasn't to be. Startlingly, surprisingly, a jeep came roaring across their front, its occupants bouncing up and down in the rough terrain like toy soldiers. Von Dodenburg could not hear what the soldiers were crying, but he knew from the frightened look on their faces that they had spotted the Tigers creeping up on the Shermans and were shouting a warning.

He grabbed the turret machine-gun. Without sighting it, he pressed the trigger angrily. Red and white tracer went racing towards the flying jeep, gathering speed with every second. The driver was hit. He slumped across the wheel, dead. The jeep went out of control. In vain the other occupants tried to fling themselves out. Too late! The jeep crashed headlong into a big oak. The bonnet crumpled and the jeep caught fire immediately. But the dead and dying Americans had done what they had come to do, for the laager was now a mass of angry, frightened, running men, grabbing their leather helmets, pulling themselves aboard the thirty-ton Shermans, starting their engines, swinging their electrically operated turrets round to meet the German challenge.

'*Heaven, arse and cloudburst*!' von Dodenburg cursed angrily and then yelled above the sudden racket. '*FEUER*!'

There was the stomach-churning spasm of the recoil, as the great 88mm cannon crashed into action. The gleaming yellow shell-case clattered smoking to the metal deck, flooding the turret with acrid choking fumes, as the shell streaked towards its target, a solid white-glowing blur.

At that range, Schulze could not miss. A Sherman staggered as if buffeted by a giant fist. Suddenly, startlingly, a brilliant silver hole had been skewered in its side. For a moment nothing happened. Then suddenly bright white fumes started to stream from its engine. 'We've hit the bugger!' Schulze cried jubilantly, as the gun-layer thrust another shell into the gaping breech. Frantically men were clambering out of the stricken tank before it ignited. But they didn't get far. Cruelly von Dodenburg pressed the trigger of the co-axial machine-gun. A stream of seven-millimetre slugs streamed towards them at a rate of 1,000 rounds a minute. They were literally sawn in half. A man caught in mid-stride seemed suspended there like the statue of a runner, blood jetting from multiple wounds as if from a sieve. Another fell, throwing up his arms in absolute agony to flop down a moment later, body hiccuping convulsively. Next moment the Sherman's highly volatile petrol engine exploded and they disappeared in a blinding sheet of yellow flame.

Now the Tigers' guns were thundering everywhere, slamming shell after shell into the Shermans, their drivers furiously revving their engines in their haste to escape the massacre.

Tank after tank went up in flames. Now there were at least a score of them blazing furiously, their crews running for their lives only to be mown down mercilessly in that cruel hail of machine-gun fire.

'No wonder they call the friggers Ronson Lighters,' Schulze said through gritted teeth, face lathered with sweat. 'One bit of flame near them and they go right up.' He pulled the firing lever and yet again an AP shell went hurrying to knock out another Sherman.

But now some of the enemy tanks were escaping the trap. Cleverly using the cover of their stricken comrades, they were working their way round to the left flank of the stationary Tigers. Von Dodenburg yelled an urgent warning to Krings further up the line. 'Watch your left flank, Lieutenant!' he bellowed. 'They're trying to shaft you from that direction! Over and out!' He left Krings to his fate, for directly to their front, a Sherman had burst straight out of the vines in a shower of green and was advancing straight at them, big new seventeen-pounder cannon swinging round towards the Tiger. He knew immediately what the American commander would do. He would try to move to the flank of the Tigers, knowing that their glacis plates were virtually impregnable, and attempt to knock them out from the side. 'That's what you think,' he cried to no one in particular and ordered, 'Enemy tank - twelve o' clock - *fire*!'

Effortlessly Schulze swung the turret round. The Sherman slid into the bright glass circle of his lens. The cross-wires sliced it in half. He grabbed the firing lever. The gun erupted. The empty shell-case clattered to the deck. Again the turret was flooded with acrid, choking fumes. Von Dodenburg blinked and peered through the periscope.

To his front, the Sherman rocked from side to side like a child's toy, caught in a sudden wind. Oily black smoke, flecked by fiery-red sparks, billowed from its open turret. The gun sank like a broken limb and then the commander was fighting his way out of the hatch, the flames already licking greedily at his body. They swept up and enveloped him. His hair caught fire. With hands that were themselves ablaze now, he tried to beat them out, weakeningly visibly by the instant. As he crumpled to the ground, von Dodenburg caught one horrifying glimpse of the American's face turning rapidly into a charred death's head, out of which the teeth grinned horrifically, a brilliant white.

But there was no time to concern himself with such matters now. The Americans were reacting in strength. Already he could hear the pounding of Krings' guns to the left as they fought off the Americans trying to outflank them. Self-propelled guns, armed with tremendous 105mm cannon, were also advancing on them, glimpsed through the fog of battle. Here and there, too, he caught sight of men on foot, toting long steel tubes on their shoulders and hung with rockets: bazookamen risking death to stalk the sixty-ton monsters. It was almost time, von Dodenburg knew, to withdraw.

'Matz,' he yelled above the thunder of battle, 'reverse! Move back to the cutting!' He pressed his throat-mike. 'CO to all . . . prepare to withdraw . . .'

To his left, the SPs had turned their concentrated attention on one of Krings' tanks. Three of them were firing at it from a hull-down position, pumping shell after shell at it. Somehow the Tiger survived, in spite of the fact that its hull was scarred silver in a dozen different spots where it had been struck. But von Dodenburg knew it couldn't last much longer. The Americans would get lucky in a moment and that would be that.

Desperately von Dodenburg yelled to a sweating Matz, as the Tiger's right track was severed and it flopped to the rear, effectively crippling the tank, 'Lights . . ! Flick on the lights . . . *quick*!'

Matz responded immediately. He knew the old trick too. He flicked the tank's lights on and off again. Then on one more time.

The self-propelled guns reacted as von Dodenburg expected they would. For some reason von Dodenburg had been unable to work out, enemy tanks always reacted in the same way when they saw lights; they turned their attention on to the tank which flashed them. The Americans were no different from the Russians, the British, the French before them. Immediately they began to concentrate their fire on von Dodenburg's retreating Tiger. As Schulze fired furiously at them and the crew of the crippled tank baled out and fled for safety, the huge armour-piercing shells ripped the air apart, slamming into the command tank. Time and time again it rocked as if struck by a tornado. The air stank of molten metal as they attempted to bore their way through the Tiger's thick hide. Once von Dodenburg watched with awed, horrified fascination as an enemy shell scored its way around the outside of the turret, sizzling and hissing as if with anger, trying to penetrate it. It would take only a fragment, he knew, to break through and they would all be dead or horribly maimed in seconds, as the steel fragment flew from side to side bouncing off the sides of the turret. But it didn't. Instead it flew off harmlessly into the vineyards and then, as von Dodenburg slumped against the steel wall, all energy sapped, and bathed in sweat, they entered the safety of the cutting from which they had emerged to do battle in what suddenly seemed another age, though it was only ten minutes ago.

Behind them they left at least fifty crippled, burning Shermans and dead Americans everywhere sprawled out in their shorts, free to sun-bathe for eternity now. At the cost of one Tiger, they had decimated a whole American combat command. The Americans would not attack Montélimar this day.

CHAPTER 3

'*Not exactly a frigging enthusiastic welcome for us conquering frigging heroes*!' Schulze commented morosely, as they began to roll through the bomb-littered streets of Montélimar.

'What do you expect, you big horned-ox?' came Matz's funereal voice from below. 'Frigging eggs in yer beer!'

Von Dodenburg smiled wanly, while Marchant, standing next to him in the turret, glowered in that intense, red-hot manner of his at the sullen soldiers and the line of black-clad housewives lining up outside a food shop, handkerchiefs tied around their heads against the soot and ash still raining down from the last bombing attack. '*Salaud*!' he commented morosely. 'Ought to shoot the lot of them. Useless mouths to feed!'

'A very radical solution, Major,' von Dodenburg said gently, as they swung round a corner, trying to ignore the angry raised fists of the housewives.

'Radical times demand radical solutions,' Marchant answered unabashed, tapping his pistol holster significantly. 'Ever since the Revolution, our people have forgotten what discipline is. They need to be taught it again – *severely*!' He glowered.

Von Dodenburg grunted something in a non-committal sort of way and stared at the elderly field-grey so busy looting one of the wrecked buildings, arms full of stolen jars of preserves, that he did not even seem to hear the rumble of the big, battle-scarred tanks. Somehow the sight angered him. Of course he did not expect a hero's welcome, but they had just been out there, risking their skins for that fat field-grey. 'Schulze,' he snapped, 'arrest that man for looting!'

The big NCO looked at him in surprise, but said nothing. He dropped over the side of the moving tank, Schmeisser clutched in his paw like a child's toy. 'Hey, you grandad, get yer frigging thieving flippers off,' von Dodenburg heard him say, and then they were gone.

Below, Matz said a little enviously, 'You shouldn't have done that, sir. Nothing in knickers in Montélimar'll be safe this night. He'll screw anything with hair on it. They'd better take in their brooms,' he added obscurely.

Von Dodenburg smiled wanly, and wished he could live like Schulze, a simple affair of 'suds and gash', as he would have put it. But he couldn't. Behind them the American guns started to thunder again. The enemy had recovered from the shock of that surprise attack. They were reacting predictably with another artillery bombardment; undoubtedly the *Jabos* would soon follow. Suddenly he wondered how long he and Wotan would be able to take it before they too started to crack like the field-greys and the civilians . . .

'*Grossartig, mein lieber von Dodenburg*!' Hartmann hissed in that eerie manner of his, pumping the young colonel's hand with unusual energy for him. 'You really gave the *Amis* a black eye this day. You have my heartiest thanks and congratulations.'

'Thank you, sir,' von Dodenburg said, watching the silver flash of a *Jabo* falling out of the velvet evening sky, little black eggs dropping from its plump body to land on Montélimar. 'What of General Wiese and his 19th, sir?'

'They are doing very well, if you can call a retreat an achievement,' Hartmann attempted a smile and failed. Hastily he thrust back his bulging yellow false teeth which had slipped from the plastic gums. 'Excuse me, von Dodenburg. Good as our German surgeons are, the bits and pieces they have blessed me with don't always function as they should. Only the other morning I found myself pissing in five different directions at one and the same time . . . Back to Wiese. He expects the bulk of the 19th to commence passing through Lyon in two days' time. They might have trouble. Lyon has a strong Red element, but I am confident he'll make it within twenty-four hours.'

Von Dodenburg nodded his understanding. Outside, the *Jabo* pilot was throwing his Thunderbolt through a series of wild, triumphant manoeuvres as mushrooms of smoke started to ascend into the evening sky. How omnipotent those American flyboys were, von Dodenburg told himself. What concern was it of theirs that this was a French town and that there were French civilians below, too? Like naughty irresponsible schoolboys they had been let loose on Europe, with only one order – *destroy it*! Somehow it wasn't fair that they could get away with it without being punished as naughty schoolboys should. 'So we will have to hold here, sir, for at least another three days?'

'Yes, I would think that would do it.'

'And then, sir?'

Hartmann's frightening face cracked into a ghastly parody of a smile. 'That my dear, von Dodenburg, is a decidedly sticky question, indeed. As you know the *Amis* have got us pretty well bottled up here in Montélimar. They've cut the *Route Nationale* Seven to the north of us and, fools that they are, instead of trying to drive on and cut off Wiese, they remain here and besiege us. But no matter.' He dismissed that factor with a wave of his crippled hand. Outside another *Jabo* was zooming in at tree-top level for the attack.

'Once we got the order to do so, in theory, von Dodenburg, we should be able to withdraw, break through the *Ami* ring to the north, and with luck rejoin Wiese. But,' he shrugged cynically, 'with what? You and your chaps might have a fifty-fifty chance of getting out, but for me and those wretched field-greys of mine, with no transport, no heavy weapons, *and no guts*, there is no hope.' He sighed a little wearily. 'For me and them there are two possibilities – to die in battle or to surrender. What does it all matter?' His one eye bore into the younger officer's face. 'We've lost the war, it's obvious, isn't it?'

Von Dodenburg was shocked. The writing was on the wall for the Third Reich in this terrible summer of 1944, he knew that, but to hear a police general and member of the SS openly state that Germany had lost was more than a surprise. 'I know we have suffered many defeats, sir,' von Dodenburg stuttered. 'In Normandy and in the East, but there is much talk of our new secret weapons . . . and the fact that the Western Allies are already quarrelling among themselves.'

'*Pap*!' Hartmann dismissed his argument contemptuously. 'Pap, von Dodenburg, sugar titty put out by the Poison Dwarf in Berlin to appease the masses. But no matter, let us forget that. We shall do our duty, von Dodenburg, and hold out another three days here and then,' he shrugged again, voice full of cynicism and resignation, 'we surrender or . . . *we die here*!'

There was a finality about his words which precluded any further discussion. So they sat there, the two of them in the darkening room, listening to the sound of the *Jabo's* engine dying away, the ancient tall clock in the corner ticking away the minutes of their life with grave metallic inexorability, each one of them wrapped in a cocoon of his own thoughts, but both knowing that the die had been cast. They had three more days to fight – *and live* . . .

'*We'd rather fuck than fight*!' Schulze bellowed drunkenly, not a kilometre away from where the two officers now sat and brooded. The fat field-grey's loot had proved very valuable indeed. While he now languished in jail, cursing the day that he had decided he could do a 'little organizing', – 'finding something before it was lost', as the stubble-hoppers called looting, Sergeant Schulze had quickly transformed the stolen jewellery into something that appealed more to his loving, generous nature. Two bottles of black market brandy, a dozen French contraceptives, and the name of a certain *etablissement*, where there were '*beaucoup* girls', a lot of '*zig-zig*' and even more '*jig-jig*'.

Now Schulze and Matz staggered through the blacked-out streets, dodging the MP patrols wherever they spotted them, heading for the 'sauce and the gash', as Schulze chortled in his usual poetic manner.

Five minutes later they found the place which would provide those delights. Their noses told them they were at the right place even before they threw open the door of the cellar. '*Gash*!' Matz cried joyfully. 'I can smell it from here, real hot juicy female gash!' He tugged his arm from Schulze's and broke into an awkward run, his artificial leg creaking audibly, heading for the cellar door from which came a faint chink of yellow light and the muted sound of music.

Schulze stumbled after him and threw it open to breathe in awe, 'Oh my God, *paradise*, Matz!'

Matz stumbled to a halt next to him and said, 'More like frigging ladies' night in the local Turkish bath!'

The cellar, thick with blue cigarette-smoke and heavy with the smell of cheap perfume and cognac, was piled high with black market goods, crate upon crate of them, between which, sprawled on silken cushions, were the whores, all drunk and clad in bright, gaudy artificial silk underwear, listening to an ancient gramophone playing a squeaky version of '*J'attendrai*'.

'Cor, fuck a little pig!' Schulze whispered emotionally, suddenly overcome by the awesome sight of so much naked female flesh. 'I'd like to fill *their* teeth one by one – *slowly*!' He emphasized the power of his feelings by making a determined grab for his bulging crotch. 'Kiss me, Matzi,' he simpered. 'I think I've just gone and fallen in love!'

'*Cherie*!' A huge woman in black knickers and net stockings, but otherwise naked, flung herself at Matz. His knee-joint creaked audibly as he took that tremendous weight, her breasts smothering his wizened face. 'Christ,' he gasped, half suffocating, 'she's trying to poke out my optics with her tits! *Save me* . . .' He disappeared between those huge dugs, gasping pleasurably.

Schulze's eyes gleamed greedily as another of the drunken whores advanced upon him, her breasts trembling like jellies under the flimsy material of her sheer black négligé. 'I'm gonna die a frigging happy man,' he breathed, while down on the floor, swamped by the half-naked woman, Matz cried desperately, 'Hey *not that*! woman. *That's my frigging wooden leg* . . . Schulze, tell the silly cow she's got hold of the wrong thing.'

But Schulze had no time for the unfortunate mix-up on the floor. For not only was the whore in the sheer black négligé advancing upon him making encouraging noises, but another one had joined her, a great black mare of a woman, clad in sky-blue knickers and nothing else. Her dark eyes flashing, she cried, '*Jig-jig*, German soldier want lot *jig-jig*?' She made an explicit, if obscene, gesture with her clenched fist. Schulze's eyes nearly popped out of his head. 'Two of them,' he cried, 'two great pieces of steaming gash, all for Frau Schulze's handsome son!' Hastily be began to fumble with his flies, while with his other paw he ripped at the packet of contraceptives, exclaiming, 'Only a dozen . . . I wonder if it's gonna be enough?'

Down on the floor, Matz came up for air momentarily, face crimson, gasping, 'I think I'm gonna die, Schulzi . . . But I'll die a happy man –' He disappeared again, just as Schulze put his arm round the first of the whores, yelling proudly, 'Now just look what Sergeant Schulze has gone and brought yer as a present!'

'*Oh, la la*!' the whore simpered, feigning shock at the sight, '*quelle horreur*!'

'That's not a horror,' Schulze chortled, 'that is a real genuine one hundred per cent diamond cutter, a real blue-veiner, and *cherie*, you and your friend are gonna have the privilege, the rare privilege, of being serviced by Sergeant Schulze's celebrated diamond cutter this very night!' Grandly he flung out his other arm to encompass the black mare in the sky-blue knickers and declared, 'But let us not waste a moment's precious time. Let us to bed and I will show you what delights this night holds for you two darling girls.'

But Sergeant Schulze was not fated to grant the two drunken, giggling whores the 'rare privilege' of his 'celebrated diamond cutter' this night, nor for some nights to come for that matter.

In the very same instant that he started for the stairs with the two whores, there came a thunderous knock on the door of the cellar and a harsh official voice bellowed, '*Alle raus aus dem puff*! *Los . . . los . . . los . . . Raus . . . Wird's bald*!'

There was a crash and suddenly a huge sergeant of military police was standing there, the silver crescent of his authority dangling from his neck, his hands clasping a loaded carbine. He glowered at Schulze and barked, 'Get your mitts off'n that lady's tits, Sergeant!'

Schulze stared at him in bewilderment and at the other MPs crowding in behind him, their eyes taking in the sight of the naked whores greedily. 'What's going on?' he demanded stupidly. 'Where's the fire, comrade? Can't a soldier cock his leg over without –'

'The Amis have broken through!' the big chain-dog interrupted him harshly! 'They're coming right up the main *Route Nationale* Seven. Can't you hear the guns?' He indicated to the south where the sky was flushed a bright pink and urgent flares signalling for help were soaring into the night sky. 'Everybody and his frigging son is needed at the front.' He laughed coarsely. 'So put away that dong, soldier – double-quick time now. There's gonna be no fucking for you tonight . . . *just fighting* . . .'

CHAPTER 4

The night was chaos. The whole horizon was ablaze. Later the defenders, those who survived, would learn that the Americans were bombarding Montélimar with over four hundred guns at close range. Now a furious fire had descended upon the city, as salvo after salvo ripped it apart. Dismembered bodies flew everywhere, the smoking rubble splashed a bright red with the blood of the victims, soldiers and civilians alike. As the column of tanks and half-tracks forced its way through the shattered streets, there were men and women writhing in agony in the gutters on all sides.

Vicious purple tongues of flame leaped up from the shattered rooftops. Weakened buildings collapsed and came racing down in a mad flurry of masonry. Apartment buildings shivered and shook like theatrical scenery. All was chaos and destruction.

A column of horse-drawn 'goulash cannon', as the stubble-hoppers called the mobile food-boilers, fleeing from the front, was straddled by a tremendous salvo only metres away from the Wotan's tanks. Horses and men went down on all sides. Steaming hot pea-soup flooded the body-littered gutters. Crazed horses, their tails and manes blazing a fiery red, stampeded down the street, dragging their shattered carts after them.

As if by magic, old women appeared from the smoking ruins, knives and pails at the ready. '*Fresh meat*!' they chanted hysterically, flinging themselves at the dying nags, cutting and slashing at the writhing beasts like the furies, their skinny arms a blood-red right up to the elbows.

A trickle of field-greys, wild-eyed and staring, their weapons long flung away, shambled down the street, crying, 'They're coming . . . They're right behind us . . . *They're coming*!' Somewhere a machine-gun opened up angrily.

Whether it was friend or foe, the advancing Wotan men had no time to find out. They were needed at the front. The deserters went down in a mess of crazily flailing arms and legs, screaming in agony. Next instant the big tracks were rolling over their bodies, pulping them into a blood-red gore. The column clattered on . . .

'Stop the fighting . . . Surrender now before it's too late!' they cried, as the column rolled towards the *Route Nationale*. '*À bas les allemands*!' Here and there the bolder of the civilians, men, women and children, working people for the most part to judge by their poor clothes, shook their fists at the passing tanks or gave the clenched-fist salute of the communists. From an upper window there came the bright-red flash of a rifle. One of the Tiger gunners didn't hesitate. He pressed the trigger of his co-axial machine gun. Lead scythed the upper window. A body came flying out to slap onto the cobbles below. The protesting crowd broke and fled in sudden panic.

Now von Dodenberg, up in the tank at point, could see the advancing *Amis* quite clearly. A column of Shermans were coming down the main road, firing smoke as they advanced, though not very effectively. In the houses and gardens on both sides of the road, infantry were dodging in and out in little groups, bayonets fixed, throwing grenades, snapping off individual shots, clearing house after house.

Von Dodenburg took in the situation immediately. He raised his hand to signal the others to stop. Opposite in a shattered school hall, its wall gone, du Pres was standing in front of his kneeling grenadiers, each man a walking arsenal, his one hand raised in the sign of the cross. He was blessing them before they went into action.

In spite of the urgency of the moment, von Dodenburg was touched. Without their helmets, and kneeling in the debris, du Pres's grenadiers looked absurdly young and innocent. For a second or two, von Dodenburg wondered how it must be to be fighting in France for the enemy against your would-be liberators. Suddenly he realized there was no hope for du Pres and his soldiers. They would be dead men, one way or the other, sooner or later. He dismissed them and concentrated on the task at hand.

'Schulze,' he barked above the snap-and-crackle of small-arms fire further up the street, as the last field-greys either surrendered or died in the little houses.

'Sir?'

'Keep the Tigers here. I'm not risking them with those *Ami* infantry everywhere up there. You'll take your orders from Lieutenant Krings.'

Schulze looked worried, but not for himself. 'Begging your pardon, sir, but what are you going to do?'

'Going to earn my pay this morning. Major du Pres's grenadiers will take the right of the street.' Hastily von Dodenburg took a couple of grenades from the rack and shoved them down the side of his right boot. 'I'll take our chaps and tackle the left one.'

'Dicey, sir,' Schulze warned.

Von Dodenburg smiled at him. 'Crossing the street is dicey, Schulze. Now you look after my Tigers.' He slapped the turret hard. 'One day these babies are going to be our insurance policy.' With that he dropped from the tank and waved for the panzer grenadiers to dismount from the half-tracks.

Schulze shrugged and then signalled for the tanks to disperse. The drivers revved their engines hurriedly and swinging left and right from the road, smashed into the nearest houses without the slightest hesitation. Walls crumbled. Bricks came showering down. Windows were shattered. Almost immediately the upper decks of the metal monsters were covered with fallen masonry, as their big guns swung round to face the advancing Americans.

'Helmets on!' snapped du Pres, the priest no longer, a warrior now. He saluted formally in the slow French way and von Dodenburg acknowledged it equally formally. Hastily he explained his plan to the smaller man. Du Pres nodded and turned to his young soldiers, their faces now hard, set and fanatical under their helmets. He told them what the German had just said and then raising his voice, cried, '*Vive la France . . . vive la Division Charlemagne*!'

A hundred eager young voices took up the cry.

Von Dodenburg touched his hand to his helmet in salute and cried, carried away by that moment, '*Bon chance, soldats*!' Then du Pres was gone at the head of his doomed men. Von Dodenburg would not see him again. 'Watch those bazooka men!' he cried in warning to Schulze and then he, too, was gone, doubling into the little suburban gardens at the head of his heavily armed panzer grenadiers . . .

Schulze waited, his Tiger almost buried in rubble, the only sound the soft beat of the tank's engine and the flapping of a broken shutter somewhere in the heightening *Mistral*. Already he had spotted the point of the advancing Americans, big men in olive drab slipping cautiously in and out of the houses some two hundred metres away, springing over the rickety fences, burrowing through the sheds. But Schulze was not yet worried by the infantry; he was waiting for the tanks which would undoubtedly trundle up soon to support them.

'They look real good, don't they, Schulzi,' Matz called from below. 'Real nice soldier-boys, playing it by the book. You'd think they'd have some umpires awarding them points for the best field-craft. Get a load of that one crawling on his stomach. They ought to –'

'*Schnauze*!' Schulze cut him off brutally. 'Here come the Ronsons!' The very next instant, the first Sherman nosed its way hesitantly round the bend in the road, a small group of tense infantrymen with fixed bayonets clustered behind it, one of them perhaps an officer, attached to the crew by the telephone link on its rump.

Schulze's finger started to whiten on the firing bar of the 88mm. 'All right, girls, on with yer frigging party frocks, ' he hissed through gritted teeth, 'the ball is about to commence . . .'

Two hundred metres away on the left flank, von Dodenburg and his grenadiers prepared to commence that celebrated lethal ball, too, as they crept ever closer to the still unsuspecting Americans busily engaged in digging-in. They would be the second wave, von Dodenburg told himself, being held in reserve in case the first wave's attack failed, which it undoubtedly would if Schulze had anything to do with it. If he and du Pres could roll up this second wave on both flanks, once the survivors of the first wave started to stream back, the whole American front might crumble. With a bit of luck a panic might result and they'd be able to kick them out of Montélimar, lock, stock and barrel, for another day at least.

'*With a bit of luck – a big bit of frigging luck*!' that old familiar cynical voice sneered at the back of his mind. '*Pal, your luck has about run out after all these frigging years*!'

He ignored the voice and raised the ugly, clumsy signal pistol above his head. Behind him the grenadiers tensed in the ditch and garden licked suddenly parched lips, their eyes abruptly anxious. They knew what was coming. Suddenly von Dodenburg remembered the old Wotan, the Wotan of the years of victory. How big and bold his men had seemed then! What risks they had taken. How they had sung as they had gone into the attack, spending their lives recklessly, their belief in the New Order and the Cause one hundred percent, fanatical. Now the 'men' he was going to lead into the attack were callow boys. Swept by a sudden anger, he pressed the trigger. The green flare sailed spluttering into the air. A crack. A burst of unreal green flame and abruptly they were out of their hiding places, crying frenzied obscenities, cheering, shouting like some football mob, carried away by mass hysteria, hurtling grenades to their front, machine-pistols chattering frantically at their hips. Von Dodenburg ran to their front, zig-zagging wildly, springing over shell-holes, the slugs cutting the air all around him. He smashed through a greenhouse in a welter of broken glass. A big swarthy American loomed up in front. He was so dark he might well have been a negro. Instinctively von Dodenburg pressed the trigger of the signal pistol, which he was still holding for some unfathomable reason. The flare exploded in the American's face. It burst in a flash of green flame and a flurry of scarlet. The man disappeared.

To the right a slow American machine-gun began to chatter like an irate woodpecker. Behind von Dodenburg his men started to go down. He swerved right, eyes searching for it. Slugs bit into the earth all around his flying feet, erupting in little angry blue spurts. *There it was*! Coming in from the slit in the cellar-wall fifty metres away. In one and the same movement, von Dodenburg ripped the grenade out of his boot, pulled the pin, and flung it. The gun disappeared in a ball of vicious, ugly yellow flame.

He ducked, chest heaving wildly, heart thumping like a trip-hammer. A grenade sailed effortlessly over his head and exploded harmlessly. He could hear the spent metal raining down on his bent helmeted head. A squat little American ran at him, yelling furiously, armed with a bayonet. He could well have been a Jap. And again von Dodenburg wondered at the multi-racialism of the Americans. He had yet to see a pure white one.

But he had no time to go any deeper into that particular problem. The little man was very determined. His slant-eyed yellow face lathered with sweat, he lunged at von Dodenburg. Hurriedly von Dodenburg dodged to one side. The man was caught off-guard. Von Dodenburg had no time to unsling his Schmeisser. Instead he kicked hard. The heavy, cruelly-studded boot rammed into the American's crotch. He went down howling, writhing back and forth, grabbing frantically for his ruined testicles. Von Dodenburg ran on . . .

'*Pour la Patrie . . . pour la belle France . . .*!' du Pres cried frantically, as the survivors of his company started to pull back, not running yet, but firing a few rounds and then retreating again, flitting from ruin to ruin, not able to break the fierce American defence. He clamped the machine-pistol to his hip the best he could and fired a burst. But still the

Americans came on, big heavy men, who outnumbered his survivors ten times over.

Desperately he fell back into some gardens littered with abandoned equipment, a wooden shed in the middle already blazing fiercely. '*À moi*!' he yelled crazily, as a couple of survivors staggered by him, eyes wide, white and wild with fear. But they did not seem to hear and stumbled on.

Now the leading Americans were a matter of metres away. He crouched, panting hard as if he had just run a long race. He knew that if he couldn't restore this flank, von Dodenburg in the fields on the other flank would have to pull back too, if he didn't want the Americans to overrun his positions. But what he could do was little. Sell his own life? Try to hold them off with what few resources were available? He flung his last grenade at the first of the Americans. They went to ground in some rubble and for a moment he had a respite.

Du Pres bent his head, though he did not close his eyes, and whispered a prayer for guidance and succour to his God. But God was looking the other way this day. The lone bullet slammed into his side with startling suddenness. What felt like a red-hot poker bored into his thigh and he fell over, as helpless as a child, with suddenly no feeling in the whole right side of his body.

For a moment he blacked out, red and silver stars exploding in front of his closed eyes. He felt something hard beneath him – perhaps the muzzle of a rifle – and his body was lifted for an instant. Still he could not open his eyes.

'Dead!' a hard voice grunted.

'Better check the cunt's not fooling,' another voice rasped. 'Kick the Kraut in the nuts!'

'But he's a priest. I can see it from his insignia,' the first voice protested.

'Yeah, a Kraut priest. They're diff –'

There was the sudden high-pitched burst of machine-gun fire and the voice ended in a shriek of pain. Du Pres felt himself falling to the ground again and something very heavy dropped on to his body with a crash. He blacked out again.

The next thing he felt was the sensation of being dragged roughly across the bumpy ground, his uniform damp and sticky with congealed blood, with all around him angry voices mumbling in French.

He groaned and received a kick for his pains. He tried to open his eye. Unsuccessfully. His face had already been beaten to a pulp. All he could see through the teary blur was angry faces staring down at him. Someone cursed, '*Sale con*!' and spat right into his one eye. He closed it again quickly and blacked out once again . . .

He came to again to face a mob of screaming women. Fat housewives in dark ugly clothes: plain immature girls, under-nourished and pale-faced; nuns in great sweeping headdresses, 'white swans' they had called them when he had been a young man in the seminary; grannies in rustic black dresses coming down to their ankles – and all of them shrieking and screaming at him, waving their fists, spitting in his face, their hands greedily ripping off his blood-stained uniform. Already those at the back were brandishing their knifes, the great curved bread-saws that the country women used on their hard homemade bread.

A wave of absolute fear swept through the *Abbe*'s skinny, tortured body, the one side black with clotted blood. They were going to emasculate him! It was the Red rabble's standard ritual with captured enemies of the right. But as quickly as the fear had come, it vanished. Abruptly he felt perfectly calm and at peace with the world. He closed his one eye, as if in prayer. He felt his organ seized roughly and the first red-hot bite of the saw on the flesh. He bit his bottom lip until the blood came. This is how the early Christian martyrs must have felt, he told himself. '*Ma pauvre France* . . .' he whispered, and then he died.

Now von Dodenburg knew it was no use. The right flank had given. The few survivors of du Pres's Charlemagne were streaming back, crying, '*Sauve qui peut* . . . *Sauve qui peut*!' But behind them the *Amis* were moving up in force. Through the drifting smoke and the flames of the burning houses, he could ee the Shermans advancing too. Scores of them, with tight ittle clusters of infantry packed to their rear. Wotan was outnumbered mightily and now even the Tigers would not be able to save his tiny force if he did not pull back swiftly. Wearily, he raised the flare pistol to give the signal to withdraw, all energy drained from him as if a tap had been opened. The *Amis* were in Montélimar to stay. It could only be a matter of hours now. He fired the flare. It exploded above his upraised face, transforming it into a blood-red glowing death's head, and then they were running . . . running for their very lives . . .

CHAPTER 5

Now the centre of Montélimar became a graveyard for Hartmann's field-greys and Marchant's *Milice* as they fought desperately to stop the Americans advancing any further up that vital *Route Nationale* Seven leading north. The foxholes burrowed into the *pavé* and in the rubble of wrecked stores were heaped with their bodies. When the bemused survivors stood upon them during a lull in the firing, eerie cries escaped from their open mouths, as if they were still alive - the hot August sun had had its effect on their bloated, gas-filled bellies. Rats the size of cats were everywhere, feasting on the dead, and the wounded were given pistols to ward them off. If they fell asleep, they found the ugly black beasts gnawing at their toes, their fingers, even their noses.

Now that whole ugly lunar landscape was heavy with the sickly sweet stench of the dead and dying. Those who could still stand warded off the terrible cloying stink with handkerchiefs and dirty rags doused in looted cognac. Otherwise they would retch for hours on end with dry, body-racking sobs that left them green, weak, and shaken so that they moved around among the smoking rubble like sick old men.

The tributary of the Rhône, their sole source of water, which ran through the centre of the town, was captured by the Americans. Its course blocked with the bloated bodies of Americans, Frenchmen, and Germans. Now they drank the stagnant green-scummed water left in the lavatory cisterns and water-tanks, greedily gulping down the rust-red water from the radiators of shattered vehicles while the bullets whistled all around them. Their food began to run out and the few supply sergeants who braved the front were forced to fling cans of meat to the men in their individual foxholes. When that failed, they risked their lives to loot the dead Americans of their C-rations.

And all the time the American mortarmen poured a relentless fire down upon them, transforming the town centre of Montélimar into something which was as remote from the world they had once known as the moon. Hour after hour that tremendous barrage of howling bombs continued, a monstrous Wagnerian cacophony of doom. Men went mad. They sprang from their foxholes, bared their chests in full view of the Americans dug in only metres away crying, the froth foaming at the corners of their parched lips, '*Kill me . . . FOR GOD'S SAKE – KILL ME!*'

Others made different exits: the wrists slit with a blunt razorblade; the toe wedged inside the trigger of the rifle, the muzzle propped under the chin. It didn't matter. There was no rear for the wounded now. The regimental surgeon of Wotan had already shot himself hours before.

Horror upon horror. Krings, staggering to the rear through the smoking rubble, dragging his pulsating guts behind him like a monstrous snake. An NCO lying in a shell-hole, slowly drowning in his own blood. Another dying as he attempted to stuff his intestines back into his shattered belly, his arms thick with caked blood right up to the elbows. A head stuffed into a German helmet being thrown at the defenders by an American with a sense of humour . . . Horror after horror without end.

And all the time that tremendous barrage swept the defenders' positions relentlessly, cruelly drenching them in its savage atavistic fury, transforming them into heaps of smoking rubble, lashing out here, there and everywhere with metallic rage, howling balefully the whole while, consuming them in great spurts of ugly scarlet flame. There seemed no end to it and, to the men crouched quaking and trembling like leaves in the bottom of their shaking pits, it was as if they had never known any other life than this crazed vibrating monstrosity, spewing fire, death and destruction . . .

The sledgehammer shock of those mortar bombs, time after time, shook even von Dodenburg as he inspected the perimeter together with Marchant. He could see that the survivors were about finished. Their holes and pits were filled with their mortally wounded comrades and the churned-up ground was littered with their dead, their bodies hit over and over again by that ceaseless barrage. Even the living looked like corpses. Their faces were blanched and pinched, their lips trembling and quivering all the time, and their eyes were coated by a damp sheen, as if they were very close to tears.

'Bad,' Marchant commented, before the two of them ducked as yet another salvo of the damned mortars came howling out of the smoke-filled sky. 'Very bad.'

Von Dodenburg nodded grimly, as he watched a corporal crawling on shattered stumps a few metres away, whimpering like a trapped animal and pleading with those around to shoot him. 'Goddamit,' he burst out angrily, fists clenched in impotent rage, 'will they never stop firing those bloody mortars?'

Marchant patted him on the shoulder gently; for the fire had gone from even Marchant now. He was strangely quiet, almost resigned. 'They'll stop,' he said softly. 'That they will – when we're dead.'

Von Dodenburg bit his bottom lip, but said nothing. Together they clambered up a small hill of rubble, listening to the ping of shrapnel from the shattered, grotesquely twisted girders. The hole on top was held by a handful of field-greys. But they were finished. They had taken too much shelling, seen too many of their comrades killed violently. Now their ashen-grey faces were blank of any emotion; but their twitching lips and dilated, blank-staring eyes revealed all. One of them had evacuated his bowels in his overwhelming fear and the stench was horrific. But none of the others seemed to notice it.

Together they flung themselves down as yet another mortar bomb whistled down to explode only metres away, showering their helmets with dirt and gravel. Von Dodenburg cursed and crawled up to the edge of the pit, where he focused his glasses carefully, shading them so that they did not reflect any light for any waiting enemy sniper. Marchant did the same. In the pit the broken field-greys did not even notice. They continued to crouch there, trembling all the while, making strange little animal sounds.

Von Dodenburg surveyed the area. A corpse sliced in half, an apparently endless coil of intestines lying in front of it. A woman, her head gone, her skirts thrown apart carelessly to reveal her dark sex. A burned-out half-track, the dead crew still sitting bolt-upright, their faces green and purple with decay. Von Dodenburg forced himself not to think about the horrors. He fought to retain control of himself. He could not allow himself to become like these quivering wretches. Somehow there had to be a solution, at least for *his* men. Why should they be butchered like dumb animals? *Gott in Himmel*, he cursed to himself. *There has to be a way out*!

'They've moved up two mortars over there, *Obersturmbannführer*,' Marchant broke into his bitter, confused thoughts. 'In that store window – at two o'clock!'

Von Dodenburg turned in the direction in which Marchant was pointing. The Frenchman was right. He could see the little puffs of white smoke, followed by the usual obscene belch of a mortar coming from behind a pile of rubble in what had once been a large department store. Behind he could just glimpse men lugging up more bombs. 'Yes, I see it.' He shrugged. 'But they are only two of many, Marchant.'

'Of course, Colonel,' Marchant said in that strange new calm manner of his. 'But I think I and my men – what's left of them – would prefer to die taking those two out than just waiting here like dumb animals to be slaughtered.'

Von Dodenburg looked at Marchant's dark, unshaven face, as if he were seeing it for the very first time. 'Do you mean that?'

'*Bien sûr*,' he answered with a shrug. 'There is no more hope for us. We shall never escape Montélimar.' He forced a weary smile. 'Have I not always said – march or die? We have marched a long way. Now the time has come to . . . *die*!' Without waiting to see von Dodenburg's reaction to his final statement, he tugged at the whistle hanging from his lapel. He shrilled it three times, drowning out even the barrage. '*Battalion Marchant*,' he called, 'on your feet! Battalion Marchant – *attend*!'

A man in the dark-blue uniform of the *Milice* rose from the rubble to the right. Another followed. And another. Like grey ghosts rising from the grave, they lifted themselves up silently and waited. Marchant didn't hesitate. He gave von Dodenburg that old slow salute of the *Legion Etrangère*, smiled bleakly and turned. His men raised their weapons while Marchant drew his pistol with slow purposefulness. 'Battalion Marchant,' he cried, '*Battalion Marchant will advance*!'

Slowly, almost thoughtfully, the handful of survivors began to advance through the smoking rubble, bodies bent slightly as if against driving rain, ignoring the din, the explosions which leaped about them, the rising angry crackle of small-arms fire.

Marchant pushed his way to the head of the thin line, *kepi* set at a bold angle on his cropped head, cigarette crooked out of the side of his mouth, a thin wisp of smoke rising over his right shoulder.

Von Dodenburg watched them go, knowing what they were feeling, that mood of unutterable loneliness, the sense of timeless unreality, the feeling of total desolation, mixed with a strange wild urge, a desire for death that was almost sexual in its intensity.

'*Marchez ou crevez*!' Marchant cried abruptly, his voice booming over the roar of the bombardment.

Suddenly, surprisingly, they were stumbling into a weary shuffle, bayonets gleaming, going to their deaths.

'*Marchez ou crevez*!' Marchant called one last time and then the machine-guns began to sing that old brutal song of death and the fog of war swallowed them up, leaving behind that coarse unfeeling echo. '*March or die . . .*'

CHAPTER 6

Hartmann handed von Dodenburg the glass. 'Cognac,' he rasped in that strange voice of his. 'Drink it. You look if you could use it.'

Wordlessly von Dodenburg nodded his thanks and drained the glass, grateful for the sudden energy it generated in his worn body. Outside, the American machine-gunners were scything Hartmann's headquarters with tracer. Plaster and brickwork flew everywhere and the air coming through the shattered window was acrid with the stink of burnt cordite. Hartmann did not even notice. He waited until the younger officer had put down his glass before hissing, 'Well, now we have the gravy, as you stubble-hoppers call it, and it's a damned fine gravy at that!' He grunted and shoved back his dislodged teeth automatically.

'Is the clock really in the pisspot, sir?' Von Dodenburg was too tired, too despondent this afternoon, to observe the niceties of civilized behaviour between senior officers.

'Yes, definitely!' Hartmann slapped the piece of paper in front of him on the littered desk. 'Signal from General Wiese. While we've been holding here, the French have slipped a division up the left bank of the Rhône right into Northern France.' He looked hard at von Dodenburg. 'This morning at zero eight hundred, they linked up with the Americans breaking out of their Normandy bridgehead at Chantilly. General Wiese's 19th Army has missed the boat. According to his signal, he is now turning east through the Belfort Gap, heading for Alsace.'

Von Dodenburg felt utterly defeated as he visualized the geography of France and realised the full import of that signal. 'You mean that there will be no great counter-attack in Normandy, sir?' he said.

'Exactly.'

'And everything we have done here, all the death, all the suffering,' von Dodenburg stuttered, while outside the machine-gun bullets ripped up the wall, 'has been in vain . . . *to no purpose* . . . ?'

Hartmann nodded solemnly.

'Marchant . . . du Pres . . . and all my young men . . . they died quite purposelessly . . . ?' von Dodenburg stopped abruptly, staring at the dirty wallpaper opposite as if it were of some considerable interest.

Hartmann nodded again and said, 'It has always been that way in war, von Dodenburg. Once, back in the good days, you shared Germany's triumphs. But those same triumphs were of no substance. They led to Germany's defeats, and what will be the purpose of Germany's defeats? Will they be the end of our Homeland?' He shook his head slowly. 'Of course not! Germany is much too important to be allowed by the victors to go under. But in 1944 we can only think of defeat and what we can save out of the débâcle.'

'*Save*?' von Dodenburg echoed stupidly.

'Yes, *save*! You have a duty – now that we know the worst – only to yourself and your men.'

'I don't understand, sir.'

'The defence of "Nougat City" is already history,' he chuckled in that eerie manner of his, his lopsided head held at an angle to prevent his false teeth slipping out of his ruined mouth, 'A mere footnote – one day – in the history books of World War Two. So now, von Dodenburg, you must think of yourself and your regiment, SS Assault Regiment Wotan. No more of their lives must be spent needlessly here in Montélimar.'

'But there is no way out, sir. The *Amis* have the place sewn up. We either die here or surrender,' von Dodenburg said with a note of near despair in his voice.

'Not quite,' Hartmann said carefully, one eye twinkling a little. 'The *Amis* have got the road system tied up admittedly, and the Rhône waterway, too. But they have – surprisingly, I must say – forgotten one means of transport out of the city heading north.'

Von Dodenburg felt his exhausted lethargy beginning to leave him. He sensed the first faint stirrings of new hope. Was there a way out for him and Wotan after all? Perhaps there was a chance that they might not have to waste their young lives here in Montélimar to no purpose. 'Do you mean there is a way out, sir?' he asked, suddenly strength in his voice once more, the machine-gunning forgotten now.

'I think so. You know before the Führer took power in Thirty-three I was a cop, a sergeant of detectives in fact. And professional cops are survivors. They always look for a way out. Policemen don't like dying a hero's death. So at the start of the battle here, I ensured there would be a way out for *General der Polizei und SS* Hartmann, in the form of a train, an armoured train at that.'

'What?' von Dodenburg exclaimed with surprise.

'Yes, it used to belong to Marshal Petain* before he decided it would be wiser for him to spend his old age in the Reich. I appropriated it and now, my dear von Dodenburg, that same train, fuelled up, together with a reliable German driver and fireman, is currently sheltered in the shunting yard not a million kilometres from here. And von Dodenburg, you and your brave young men are going to make use of that train to escape from this hell-hole before it is too late. After the war, our Homeland will have much need of young men like yours.'

'But how can we . . . I mean, the place is surrounded?' von Dodenburg stuttered helplessly, a dozen different objections springing to mind immediately.

Hartmann held up his blackened claw for silence. 'My field-greys and I are dead men already,' he said flatly, as if it were a matter of fact, unworthy of any further discussion. 'They are old, worn-out, born losers. They will be of no use to

* Ruler of Vichy France, which collaborated with Nazi Germany in WWII

Germany once we have lost this war. But they will serve some useful purpose if they help to save the lives of you and your men. One last diversion, while you, *mein lieber* von Dodenburg, make a run for it.' He paused momentarily and gazed at von Dodenburg with that terrible face of his, the glass eye still staring ahead fixedly, but with something akin to a sad warmth in the other. '*Obersturmbannführer* von Dodenburg,' he said solemnly, 'the time has come for you and your men to learn not how to *die* for Germany, but how to *live* for it! Now listen, this is my plan . . .'

It was a strange night, full of alarms and sudden frights. The bombardment had ceased now. In the darkness the American mortarmen were afraid of hitting their own infantry, dug in only yards from the last German positions. But on all sides the small-arms duel continued, the darkness split by the sudden flash of rifle fire and the hiss of red tracer like the flight of a myriad angry hornets. And over the American lines flares, red, green and silver, kept shooting into the night sky, as if the dug-in GIs half-suspected that all was not as it should be in the German positions. On both sides there was a feeling of electric tension so that the least movement, the collapse of yet another shell-weakened wall, or even the stirring of the *Mistral* in the shattered houses, would bring long bursts of frightened machine-gun fire.

'Shoot first and ask questions afterwards,' Hartmann said, as he and von Dodenburg crouched together in the glowing ruins, observing the American positions.

Von Dodenburg nodded, but said nothing, tensing for the first sound of the Tiger engines starting up. That would undoubtedly be the signal for the American lines to erupt with fire. Thereafter it would be in God's hands. Those two hundred metres to the shunting yard and the waiting train might well be two hundred kilometres, two thousand for that matter.

Hartmann tugged at his helmet and said, 'I shall be glad

when it's all over. All these years, the struggle for power in the twenties, the rebirth in the thirties, the war, my wounds.' He sighed. 'They've all taken their toll. Quite frankly, von Dodenburg, I shall be glad to die.'

Still the other man remained silent. With one ear cocked for the first sound of the motors, he ran the plan through his mind once more. As soon as the firing started, Hartmann would lead his field-greys forward in one last suicidal charge. Conveniently he had placed half a dozen chain-dogs, armed with machine-guns, to their rear to ensure that they did exactly that. For its part, Wotan would break out to the left, racing for the railway station where the locomotive was in the shed, ready to move out at a moment's notice. The catch was that the armoured force would have to run the length of the *Ami* line to make their escape; and in the darkness and the confused mess of the shell-shattered streets, it would only take one brave bazookaman to knock out the lead tank and hold up the whole column. What would happen then was easily predictable; it would be mass slaughter. SS Assault Regiment Wotan would cease to exist.

Hartmann seemed to be able to read von Dodenburg's gloomy thoughts; for he said: 'It will work, *Obersturmbannführer*, I feel it in my ancient bones. Of course, you might lose some of your men, but the *gros* will get through, no fear. The Americans, young nation as they may be, are rigid, inflexible in their thinking. Look how they have battered their heads bloody here at Montélimar for no real purpose.'

'Let's hope you're right, sir,' von Dodenburg answered, still straining his ears.

A star shell exploded over the enemy positions in a burst of brilliant silver flame. For an instant von Dodenburg was blinded and then he could see the *Amis* holes everywhere lining the debris-littered street they would have to take. He frowned. It was going to be hell.

Next to him, Hartmann rose to his feet, took his pistol carefully out of the holster and rasped to the waiting field-greys, their bayonets already fixed, '*Fertigmachen zum Angriff*!'

Reluctantly the middle-aged soldiers rose from their hiding places. Hartmann turned to von Dodenburg, his ruined face set and hard in that harsh silver glow. 'Good luck, von Dodenburg and,' he chuckled suddenly, 'for one last time, *Heil Hitler*!'

Von Dodenburg clicked to attention. 'Thank you sir . . . and *Heil Hitler*!'

Hartmann's single eye gleamed and he raised his pistol, von Dodenburg forgotten already in his eagerness to die and have the misery done with. '*ATTACK*!' he bellowed and hobbled forward. With a weary '*hurrah*' the field-greys rose from their holes, their bayonets glistening silver in the light of the flare. Behind them the Tigers' engines started up with a mighty roar, as the enemy machine-guns began to chatter. It was time to leave Montélimar for good . . .

CHAPTER 7

'*After me*!' von Dodenburg cried, as his lead Tiger burst out of the rubble and swung left. '*The colonel's got a hole in his arse*!'

'*FOLLOW THE CO . . .*' Schulze took up that wild cry, as the firing intensified immediately. '*THE COLONEL'S GOT A HOLE IN HIS ARSE*!'

Now the whole column, Tigers in the lead, the half-tracks filled with grenadiers crouching behind the protection of the steel plates following, surged forward as Hartmann's field-greys charged the American positions in that final suicidal attack. On both sides the houses spat fire. Bullets spattered off the armour like heavy tropical rain on a tin roof. An AP shell shrieked, a white-glowing blur, towards von Dodenburg's Tiger. He ducked instinctively and it slammed against the side to go howling off into the darkness, leaving the stink of molten metal behind it . . .

Now in the glowing darkness, with the flames leaping higher and higher, von Dodenburg could just make out the shattered, spiked outline of the shunting yards. But there was still one hundred and fifty metres to go and the *Amis* seemed to be springing out of their rat-holes on all sides. A man ran into the centre of the street, that dreaded long shape bouncing up and down on his shoulder. Behind him came another American, laden with bombs. Already he was fumbling with the first one, while the bazookaman crouched, ready to fire. Von Dodenburg didn't give him a chance. Savagely, desperately, he pressed the trigger of the co-axial machine-gun. The bazookaman flung up his hands, clawing the air as if he were climbing the rungs of an invisible ladder. A moment later he and his comrade had disappeared – screaming – beneath the flailing tracks of the Tiger . . .

Another hundred metres. Behind the Tigers one of the half-tracks had been hit now. Burning fiercely, what looked like a gigantic blow-torch searing its decks, it had slewed to one side helplessly, spilling out grenadiers, screaming and writhing on the ground, as the greedy oil-flames consumed them. 'Oh, my poor boys!' von Dodenburg agonized, the tears springing to his red-rimmed eyes.

A phosphorus grenade exploded against the side of the Tiger. It burst into a sheet of dazzling white flame. Von Dodenburg was blinded. Instinctively the driver below hit the brakes. The Tiger shuddered to a stop, its tracks slithering and sending it skidding to the right. 'In three devils' name!' von Dodenburg shrieked. 'Move it –'

But it was already too late. The first AP shell slammed into the stationary monster. Von Dodenburg reeled back against the turret, while below, the sweating driver frantically attempted to start his stalled motor. Behind, the column began to come to a halt bunching dangerously, as the *Amis* concentrated their fire on the lead tank.

Angry scarlet flame stabbed the night. The rocket hurtled towards the Tiger, trailing fiery-red sparks behind it. A desperate, half-blinded von Dodenburg tensed. It was a bazooka round and at this range, even a two-inch bazooka shell could penetrate the Tiger's thick skin. There was a banshee-like shriek. Von Dodenburg prayed fervently. He felt the heat, a searing rush of angry flame, and the rocket was sailing by the stalled tank – *harmlessly*! But von Dodenburg knew they wouldn't have a second chance and already the stalled column was being racked by devastating enemy fire.

'Schulze,' he shrieked into the throat-mike, 'for Chrissake, knock this cunt off the road . . . *MOVE IT*!'

Schulze didn't hesitate. 'Matz!' he yelled above the tremendous, ear-splitting racket, the bullets rattling the length of the Tiger, 'you heard. Knock –'

But Matz was already revving his engine furiously, as he moved forward, trying to gather all possible speed before he struck the CO's tank. They collided with a great hollow boom of steel striking steel. Desperately, cursing madly, Matz tried to keep up the momentum.

Groaning and squeaking as if in protest, the stalled Tiger began to move. Millimetre by millimetre. The veins swelled and throbbed crazily at Matz's temples, his eyes bulging like those of a madman. 'Come on, you son-of-a-whore!' he cursed furiously. 'Come on, cunt . . . *move*! *MO* –'

The bazooka rocket slammed into the driver's compartment with a sound like the knell of doom. The driver gave one last awesome shriek as that great searing flame ripped through his legs and then he was dead and the fires were starting everywhere.

'Bale out . . . bale out . . !' von Dodenburg cried. 'Before the ammo locker explodes . . . *out* . . . *out*!'

The gunner and radioman ripped off their headphones. They vaulted out of the turret. Grimly von Dodenburg dropped into the smoke-filled driver's compartment. He shoved the legless horror to one side and kicked his severed lower body from the controls.

Matz's tank struck his own again. He steered desperately, knowing that if he lost control and blocked the road that would be the end of SS Assault Regiment Wotan. The flames were leaping higher and higher. He could hear the angry crackle of the circuits blowing and see the spurts of bright-blue flames. It could only be a matter of seconds now before they reached the ammunition locker above him.

Now they were moving once more. It was a mere five metres he needed to right the tank. Five lousy metres, it seemed like five thousand kilometres!

Sweating, raging, nerves tingling electrically, Matz reversed, slammed through the forward gears and charged. The Tiger rammed von Dodenburg's – *hard*. Sixty tons of steel powered by a 400 HP engine slammed into the crippled monster. And it worked! The first Tiger slithered right off the road. It tilted with an awesome groan of strained metal and then it was rolling over and von Dodenburg was scrambling out of the escape hatch below and running frantically for his very life just as the flames reached the ammunition locker and the small-arms ammunition started to explode in a crazy lethal firework display.

Hartmann dropped to the rubble, the burning pain in his shattered stomach almost unbearable. All around him the last of the attackers were throwing down their weapons and quavering fearfully, '*Kamerad . . . bitte nicht schiessen* . . . no shoot, comrade. . !'

A heavy boot slammed into Hartmann's ribs. He groaned with agony.

'Finish the Kraut sonavabitch off, Al,' someone called. 'The cock-sucker's had it anyway!'

'Hell no,' another voice objected. 'Look at them medals. They'd sure make swell souvenirs.' Half-blinded with pain, Hartmann caught a blurred glimpse of a dirty hand reaching down to pluck the Knight's Cross of the Iron Cross from his throat. But that wasn't to be. A hard, authoritative voice barked, 'Stop that looting, soldier! Can't you see that man's a general? Hey, you . . . you and you. Pick up this wounded Kraut and take him back to the CP. I want Intelligence to start working on him. We've got to know where those Kraut Tigers were taking off to, *pronto*!'

Helplessly, only half understanding the strangely accented English, which sounded little like the 'Oxford English' he had learned at school, but knowing that they were not going to allow him to die just yet, Hartmann felt himself being borne away by strong hands. Behind him the American colonel called urgently into his field phone, 'Do you read me . . . do you read me, you goddam jerk? Where are those Kraut tanks. . ? Do you read me, in Sam Hill's name, *do you read me. . ?*'

But the field phone remained obstinately silent; and two hundred yards away on his left flank, on this crazy August night in the ruined city, the young captain lay in the smoking rubble next to the ruined Tiger watching his life-blood drip away from his shattered legs, the squawking of the phone ignored. Around him lay his dead men, crushed by that last savage armoured attack. The Tigers had broken through. . .

Von Dodenburg made a hurried examination of the locomotive, the three sleek coaches and the little guards' van at the rear. It would be cramped, very cramped, but it looked good. The locomotive had armour four centimetres thick and was equipped with what looked like a steel cowcatcher, but shaped into a prong that would probably cut through any obstruction on the line. Its floor and that of the coaches, too, was reinforced steel so that even a large land-mine planted on the tracks would not be able to stop them. Each coach had slits instead of windows to be used as gun-ports while the guards' van, armoured as well, had a tower-like structure on its roof in which a machine-gunner could be posted to keep a look-out for partisans. As an awestruck Matz had commented on first seeing the armoured train, 'Why, it's like a frigging fort on wheels!'

But there was no time for any further examination of the train, its steam already raised, the half-naked fireman busy shovelling yet more coal into the greedy maws of the firebox. The sound of fresh firing was becoming louder and von Dodenburg could already see the first of the rear-guard slipping back down the sides of the burning street, one by one.

'All right,' he commanded above the noise of escaping steam, as the anxious driver opened the throttle and the wheels clattered noisily on the steel track, impatient to be off before it was too late, 'Schulze, destroy the vehicles. On the double now!'

'Sir,' Schulze barked and cupping his big paws around his mouth, he bellowed, 'Light the arse-paper, lads!'

His men did not need any urging. As one they doubled the length of the long strips of lavatory paper leading from the open fuel tanks of the Tigers and half-tracks, dousing the coarse crêpe paper with petrol from the jerricans they were holding; while at the far end other soldiers were poised with lit matches or their cigarette-lighters, waiting to ignite the primitive fuses.

Von Dodenburg turned his attention to the brawny driver, dressed in the shabby, oily dark-blue of the *Reichsbahn**, though he had a big old-fashioned revolver poked into his belt. 'Enough fuel?' he rapped.

'Yessir. To get us beyond Lyon at least . . . and water enough too, sir.'

'What about protection for yourselves? I can post a machine-gunner behind you on the tender.'

'Sandbags, sir. As soon as we get rolling, we'll put the sandbags up at each side of the cab and the loco itself is armoured. We'll be as snug as a bug in a rug, won't we, Hermann?'

The half-naked fireman did not pause in his task. Instead he grinned and winked, his teeth a pearly, startling white against his soot-blackened face.

Von Dodenburg nodded his approval, as everywhere long blue touch-flames began to hurry towards the abandoned vehicles. Next to him Schulze shook his big head in wonder and said, 'Willya just look at it, sir! A million frigging Reichsmarks of government property going up in flames, just like that!' He snapped his fingers. 'Think of all the gash that would frigging well buy.'

'You just worry about keeping your outside plumbing intact to be able to enjoy that gash!' Von Dodenburg commented with a grin, as the last of the rear guard came into the shunting yard, clattering over the *pavé* at the double. 'Load 'em up – *quick*! The *Amis* can't be far off now.'

'Load up –'

There was a tremendous *whoosh* and the rest of Schulze's bellow was drowned by the horrendous noise of the first fuel tank exploding in one of the half-tracks. It started to blaze fiercely. Now vehicle after vehicle began going up in flames, as

* German railway

the grenadiers threw their kit into the coaches, the locomotive's wheels chattering and clattering impatiently.

The first group of the enemy came cautiously round the bend which led into the shunting yard, their bodies bent and tense. A Spandau* hissed into high hysterical action. The patrol was galvanized into crazy movement, all flailing arms and legs, as if they were puppets in the hands of some mad puppet-master. The survivors fled. But a harassed, sweating von Dodenburg knew it wouldn't be long before they were back and it only needed one lucky mortar bomb exploding on the tracks and they would be trapped. 'Come on, *los . . . los . . . los* . . !' he bellowed above the roar of another exploding gas tank. 'Forget the armour. *On board*!'

On all sides the impatient, purple-faced NCOs took up the cry. Men scrambled aboard anyhow. Guns were thrust hurriedly through the firing loops. Schulze heaved a machine-gunner crew into the tower above the guards' van. The hiss of escaping steam roared ever louder. The wheels rattled. The great gleaming silver pistons slid back and forth. Schulze flung a grenade at the first of another enemy patrol and swung himself effortlessly into the cab, dragging Matz behind him. Swiftly they started to pile up the sandbags on either side. The driver opened his throttle. Desperately the half-naked fireman tossed another shovelful of coal into the roaring firebox. Von Dodenburg took a last look at the shunting yards, his face mottled and suffused with the harsh gaudy light of the burning vehicles. It was like Dante's hell, he told himself, the end of the world. Violence, destruction, fire and sudden death. Then he waited no longer. He gave three shrill blasts on his whistle. It was the signal. Next moment he swung himself aboard, too.

Smoothly the armoured train began to pull out of the yard. A cloud of smoke belched from her stack. A grenade burst against the cab in a flash of angry scarlet. A face appeared at Schulze's feet. Schulze dropped the sandbag he was holding.

* Machine-gun

The American went down as if pole-axed. The green needle of the speedometer began to creep round to the right. The train began to gather speed. A wooden barrier loomed up in the scarlet gloom. The driver tugged harder at the throttle. The armoured prong smashed through it. Wood flew everywhere. A hail of slugs pattered against the cab. A last glimpse of one of the absurd posters advertising nougat which they had seen everywhere during their stay in Montélimar and then they were through, leaving the ruined suburbs behind them. Montélimar started to disappear rapidly into the night. Suddenly the energy went out of Schulze. He dropped the last sandbag into place and leaned weakly against the shaking steel wall. 'Cor fuck a duck, Matzi,' he breathed. 'Don't let's have many more like that. I've just pissed down my right leg. . .'

CHAPTER 8

'The whole frigging frog railroad system is shot, Colonel,' the big bespectacled Intelligence officer exclaimed bitterly, while in the corner the surgeon worked frantically to patch up a dying Hartmann. 'The *maquis* effectively sabotaged the signals system when we hit the beaches. So,' he shrugged, 'no one can say whether that Kraut armoured train is heading north, south, frigging east or west! We're completely in the dark about its movements.'

In the corner Hartmann moaned softly as the surgeon, racing against time, stabbed yet another hypodermic into his good arm, muttering through gritted teeth, 'Come on, you Kraut bastard . . . revive, willya!'

'But what's so important about one single Kraut, sir?' the Intelligence officer asked, staring at his CO. 'We've got thousands of the Heinie bastards in the divisional cage. One more or less won't make much difference. Besides, they destroyed their own armour. They're on the run. They pose no threat to us now.'

The colonel took the pipe he affected out of his mouth – he thought it gave him the same craggy, sour look that marked General 'Vinegar Joe' Stilwell's face all the time, and these days everyone had a trademark of some kind or other – and said, 'This Kraut is not just any Kraut, captain. Division tells me he is Colonel Kuno von Dodenburg, commander of an elite SS regiment, and above all he is a war criminal, just like that Kraut general over there. Division says he's wanted by half the countries in Europe for war crimes. And brother, you'd better believe this,' he took the corn-cob pipe out of his mouth and pointed the dripping stem at the Intelligence officer almost in accusation, 'if we screw this one up and he gets away, the shit will really hit the fan! Seventh Army will want heads to roll – *yours and mine*! You're regular army, so you know what that means.'

The Intelligence officer nodded grimly. He did. Before Pearl Harbor it had taken twenty years to make captain, and he wanted to be bird colonel before this war was finished. In the US Regular Army, you only made grades when there was a war on. 'You want me to work on the Kraut, sir?'

'Yeah,' the colonel said sucking at his pipe, jaw set and hard. 'That frigger will know where they've gone.'

'But he's dying, sir,' the Intelligence officer protested.

'So what,' the colonel sneered. 'All you need is for him to live long enough to sing like a little canary and then he can turn in his chips, as far as I am concerned. It'll save the hangman a job. And listen, Masters,' he said, lowering his voice so that the surgeon couldn't hear, 'you don't need to wear no kid gloves. Got it?'

'Got it, sir,' the Intelligence officer answered, not relishing what was to come.

'OK, I'm off,' the colonel said, knowing that it would be damned foolish for him to be present at what was going to happen next. 'Doc,' he called to the sweating surgeon, 'that's enough.'

'But he's dying, sir,' the surgeon protested, raising his head his brow glistening with sweat in the bright white light of the hissing Coleman lantern.

'So what else is new?' the Colonel asked cynically. 'Come on, no beefing. Let's make tracks.'

The Intelligence officer waited till they had gone out, then he walked over to the dying general and slowly, almost ceremoniously, began to draw on the brown leather glove he always wore on these occasions to protect his knuckles. 'All right, Kraut bastard,' he began in German, working up to that artificial rage he needed to get the adrenalin flowing, 'I'm gonna ask some simple questions and I need some simple answers – *quick*!'

*

'I was so pissed,' Schulze was saying, 'that when I came out of the inn I saw this lamp-post and challenged it to a fight. Don't just stand there, you one-eyed bastard, I sez, come out and fight!' He shook his head. 'Good old days, they were, suds and gash!' He licked his black, parched lips and watched as the fireman fried an egg on the red-hot shovel held in the roaring firebox. 'By the Great Whore of Buxtehude, where the hounds piss out of their ears, I could just go a litre of suds right now!'

'I'll buy you a barrel of best Munich suds if we ever get out of this one,' von Dodenburg's sharp, crisp voice cut into his reverie. Next moment the young colonel came slithering down from the coal tender into the swaying cab.

The two comrades snapped to attention and the fireman swallowed the fried egg in one hasty gulp, as if he were afraid the newcomer might claim his precious delicacy for himself. Schulze shot him a murderous look. That fried egg would have been just the thing to set him up for the day. After all, a senior non-commissioned officer like himself needed more food than a fireman, with all the responsibility he carried. He then forgot the fried egg and listened attentively as von Dodenburg outlined the plan for the new day.

'Listen, you two rogues. As you know, all my officers are dead or captured. You two are the last remaining old hares among the NCOs. I'm relying on you to keep the greenbeaks going, because we can't fool ourselves. We won't be able to keep these wheels for ever.' Von Dodenburg looked out of the sandbagged cab at the dawn countryside, with the mist still writhing in and out of the dewy hollows, almost as if he expected to see the enemy lurking there already. 'Sooner or later the *Amis*'ll get onto us. And if *they* don't, the *maquis* will.'

Schulze tried to cheer up an obviously very worried von Dodenburg. 'Well, sir, this mist will keep off *Ami* air recces and those damned *Jabos* of theirs. And you know yourself just how shot their railway system is. We haven't seen a station or signal box yet which has been manned.'

'Yessir,' Matz agreed, 'all the frogs have gone home to mother.' He beamed brightly.

'Who told you to speak,' Schulze rasped, 'arse-with-ears? Don't you know that the CO is talking to me, his senior non-commissioned officer?'

Von Dodenburg forced a weary smile. '*All right, my senior non-commissioned officers*, this is what I want you to do. Keep your eyes peeled for any likely spot for an ambush. A steep gradient, cutting through the hills, railway bridge and the like.'

'Peeled like a tin of Eyetie tomatoes!' Schulze said.

'You see,' von Dodenburg continued, apparently not hearing Schulze's attempt at humour, 'I've got a plan. Before they find us, SS Assault Regiment Wotan is going to disappear. But somehow we've got to have witnesses to that disappearance.' He pursed his lips thoughtfully, while the two old hares stared at him in complete bewilderment.

'Wake up, you Kraut bastard!' the Intelligence captain thundered and, taking the ration can of urine which he was using on Hartmann, he flung some more of its contents at the German's tortured face, now minus the glass eye. Hartmann came to, urine and soggy cigarette butts trickling down his face.

'Now, I want no more goddam frigging about!' Masters cried, forcing himself not to gag at the stink that now came from the German sprawled on the wet floor. 'Where is that train heading?' He slammed his gloved fist routinely into Hartmann's puffed black and blue cheek.

He moaned. 'Let me die, please,' he slurred through swollen lips, his false teeth stomped to pieces on the floor next to him. 'Just die.'

Masters grabbed him by his soaked hair and forced his eye open. 'Look at me, Kraut. Just answer that question and I'll let you die – *pronto*!' Masters' nausea grew as he stared at that horrible, mulitated face, and the stench of faeces grew overpowering. But he knew he had to have that answer. His 'bird' depended upon it. '*Now, where are they going? WHERE?*'

Hartmann thought of von Dodenburg. What had he said to him at that last meeting? *The time has come for you and your men to learn not how to die for Germany, but how to LIVE for it!*' Now von Dodenburg and his young men of Wotan would have to die, too. He sighed, unbearably weary. 'I'll tell you . . . but let me die then . . . *please*!' he sobbed, feeling the darkness already beginning to creep up on him, the mad roaring in his ears getting ever louder.

'Spit it out!' Masters cried eagerly and tugged harder. Hartmann's face creased with agony, the blood welling a bright scarlet from his bandaged wound. 'North,' he groaned, 'north . . . to Lyon.'

Masters let his head fall to the blood-soaked lino – *hard.* Even as he died, Hartmann could hear the whirring of the field telephone and the excited voice crying, '*Colonel . . . Colonel . . . we've got the mother-fuckers. .* !'

The cocky young pilot, with his overseas cap flattened and pressed to the back of his crew-cut skull, let the A-20 spotter fall out of the morning sky, his engines throttled back to virtually stalling speed. He was sure he had just spotted something moving down there in the damned ground mist, lit a milky impenetrable white by the bright sunshine streaming down. It had been one hell of a job trying to find the main railroad track leading north. Twice he had almost crashed into power cables and once he had come down to tree-top level to find the little rural station where he had finally picked it up.

Now he played the old trick. Sliding open the cockpit flap, he switched off the engine momentarily and listened hard. Nothing but the hiss of the wind. Hastily he switched on the engine. Then he tried again. Once more nothing. 'Christ on a crutch!' he cursed to himself, 'where the hell are they?'

He turned off the engine again and strained with all his might, the little light plane losing height rapidly. He was almost at tree-top level now. In seconds he would be hitting the dirt. Still he hung on. He had to find that damned elusive train. And then it was there. The rumble of a slow train ascending some kind of incline!

'*Yippee*!' he yelled exuberantly and switched on the motor at the very last moment, in the same instant that the mist parted below to reveal the camouflaged train, the gun mounted on the rear cab already spitting angry fire. But it was too late. The young pilot was already climbing rapidly, followed by the vicious red tracer, speaking excitedly into his radio mike. 'I've found the bastards . . . *I've found them*!'

Somewhere up the pot-holed, battle-littered road an 88mm was banging away like a hammer in hell. At regular intervals its hundred-pound shells slammed into the American-held village. Next to the road, the little stone house which was K Company's CP shuddered each time like a destroyer hitting a bow-wave at full speed.

Captain Kerrigan, the company commander, did not seem to notice. He belonged to the Third Infantry and the Third Infantry were tough *hombres*; they had had more casualties and won more Medals of Honor than any other outfit in the whole of US Army. Captain Kerrigan and his veterans had become used to being pounded by the Krauts; they had been at it ever since North Africa. As if oblivious, Captain Kerrigan concentrated on his map.

Deevers had called him personally to brief him on this operation and told him there would be the major's leaf and a silver star in it for him if he pulled it off successfully. Kerrigan, who had a drawer full of silver stars, had chanced his arm and asked the Commanding General of Seventh Army whether he couldn't have three days in 'Gay Paree' instead. The CG had granted his wish and now Kerrigan worked hard and fast to get those seventy-two hours with 'boocoup brandy and boocoup broads', as he had exclaimed excitedly to his second-in-command only minutes before.

In essence, the op meant breaking off contact with the German rear guard up the road, motoring thirty klicks across rough country roads and trying to bush-whack the Kraut train at the bridge across the River Isère at Pont de L'Isère.

'And remember, Hawkins,' he told his bespectacled serious second-in-command, 'the only muscle we've got is the seventy-five mounted on the half-track. Doubt if that would have much effect on an armoured train.'

'Then we've got to get there before the Krauts, sir,' Hawkins said, 'and blow the bridge, before they can cross it.'

Kerrigan rubbed his unshaven chin, his bright Irish eyes suddenly sparkling and an unholy look on his face. 'Not *before* they get to the bridge, Hawkins,' he corrected him, 'but just when they're right *in the middle* of the goddam thing! Now come on, let's take out that frigging eight-eight up there. It's giving me a frigging headache.' He grabbed his carbine. . .

CHAPTER 9

The armoured train, its speed lessened now, laboured up the steep gradient which would take it through the pass and down to the River Isère beyond. Thick smoke poured from its stack and Schulze and Matz as they crouched in the cab could hear the strain the locomotive was undergoing. In front of them the brawny fireman, muscular body glazed with sweat, laboured mightily to keep up steam.

At regular intervals, the driver, hand tensed on the throttle, kept calling nervously, 'More coal, Hermann. The gauge is falling agen!'

And Schulze knew why he was so nervous and determined to keep up their speed. The pass ahead would be an ideal place for an ambush by the *maquis.* The driver wanted to get through it as quickly as possible. He tightened his grip on his machine-pistol, peering out of the slit in the sandbags at the milky-white ground mist.

Further back in the last coach, a worried von Dodenburg was doing the same. Ever since the lone *Ami* plane had spotted them, he had known that time was running out for Wotan rapidly. Twice he had glimpsed furtive shapes out there in the mist and he didn't need a crystal ball to know who they were. Partisans, perhaps alerted by the Americans.

Von Dodenburg forced himself to concentrate on the map spread out over his knees, while around him half his men snored, off-duty, the rest manning the slits, ready for action. The most likely place for them, he told himself, was the confluence of the Rivers Rhône and Isère, where the railway crossed the Isère on a bridge. To both sides there were hills, the ones on the Isère side turning rapidly into the Pre-Alps: an ideal place to take a quick dive. But where was he going to get his witnesses to the destruction of Wotan? He did not want to lose his wheels and then find himself hounded across enemy-held France on foot. Wotan would never survive that. He frowned hard, as the speed of the train climbing the steep ascent fell more and more. . .

The attack came with startling suddenness. Abruptly there was a screeching, banging clamour. Men were thrown off their feet as the bumpers on the coaches slammed into each other. In a flash there was confusion. MCOs barked orders. Men shouted with surprise. And then there they were! Small men in floppy black berets flitting from tree to tree, glimpsed like legless ghosts in the writhing mist, little British sten-guns chattering as they shot up the stalled train, while others flung their grenades, which made a devil of a racket but bounced harmlessly off the steel plates of the coaches. Now the troopers began to fire back. A ragged volley erupted from both sides of the train and up on the roof of the guards' van the machine-gunner scythed the trees, virtually sawing one *maquis* in half. He collapsed against the splintered trees, blood jetting from multiple wounds as if from a sieve.

Von Dodenburg pushed his way through the coach, which echoed now to the snap-and-crackle of the small-arms fight, the air heavy with the stink of burnt cordite. He nodded to the grenadier guarding the door. The man flung it open. Immediately von Dodenburg scuttled up the iron ladder to the roof, slugs whining off the steel armour on all sides. Crouching low he started to balance his way to the locomotive, trying to ignore the enemy fire, his eyes straining in the mist, trying to make out what had happened up front. Suddenly he was almost flung to the ground, as with a great shudder and hiss of escaping steam the locomotive started to reverse.

Von Dodenburg balanced himself against a stanchion, guessing that something had obstructed the line and that the driver was going to charge the obstacle. A dark wolfish face appeared abruptly at the end of the far coach. Von Dodenburg raised the Schmeisser hanging from his neck and pressed the trigger automatically. The *maquis*'s face disappeared in a welter of blood. He plunged beneath the flying wheels with a terrible scream.

Again von Dodenburg was nearly flung from his perch as the train stopped abruptly. He could hear the trickle of coarse sand onto the tracks. The driver was trying to ensure that the driving wheels gripped when he started forward once more.

The *maquis* must have guessed what he was about, for they intensified their fire, coming out of the mist-wreathed trees, ripping off burst after burst of automatic fire. Grimly von Dodenburg clung there, feeling the slugs nip and rip at his uniform.

The wheels clattered. The pistons jerked back and forth. Steam jetted from the stack in a great cloud. Von Dodenburg bit his bottom lip until the blood came. *Wouldn't the damned wheels ever grip*? Now the partisans were growing ever bolder, sneaking forward into the dead ground below the firing slits, crawling beneath the boogies. It would be only a matter of minutes before they stormed the train itself. 'Come on, damn you – *move*!' von Dodenburg cursed desperately.

The train jerked. The wheels gripped and they were moving forward once more. Von Dodenburg started to balance himself along the last coach, the air thick with flying lead. Steam enveloped him for a moment. When it cleared, he could see a dark shape clambering across the heaped coal of the tender in front of him. 'Look out!' he cried fervently.

But Schulze had already seen the intruder. He clambered up onto the tender and grabbed the Frenchman. For a moment or two they wrestled furiously on the coal, swaying wildly back and forth in a dance of death. But only for moments. Schulze, the product of Hamburg's waterfront, knew all the dirty tricks. Suddenly he let go his hold. The Frenchman fell off balance. He stumbled forward, arms flailing the empty air. Schulze ducked. With all his brutal strength, he brought his helmeted head up into the unsuspecting Frenchman's face. The Frenchman howled with absolute agony and was swept off the cab by that cruel blow, as if punched by a gigantic fist. Next instant they had smashed through the barrier which had held them and were gaining speed rapidly as they started the long descent to the River Isère. Gasping as if he had just run a great race, von Dodenburg dropped into the wildly swaying cab panting, 'And now we're gonna disappear, Schulze. . .'

'Come on, come on, you jerks!' Kerrigan cried impatiently, as he held his head to the vibrating rails, 'haul ass! The Krauts can't be far off now . . . I'm goddam sure I can hear them coming.'

Above him, hanging on for dear life high above the river, the combat engineers worked from girder to girder stringing out the wire, while on the bridge itself Kerrigan's own infantrymen packed the thick wads of explosive on the stanchions, ready for the engineers to wire them up. Everywhere there was hectic activity, the men swarming back and forth across the railway bridge like worker ants.

Kerrigan bent his head to the rail once more. Now he was sure that the missing train was coming. Indeed as his ear touched the track, he could actually feel it vibrating. He flashed a look at the other side of the Isère. There the infantry and engineers had erected a rough barrier of sleepers and hastily cut-down tree trunks. He knew it wouldn't stop a locomotive at speed, but it would slow the train down; and that was exactly what he wanted. He knew that the timing of explosive charges was always difficult. He wanted the train to be in the exact centre of the three-span bridge, travelling at a snail's pace so that the sergeant in charge of the combat engineers couldn't miss. 'Okay, Reeves,' he called to the man as he crouched over his detonator box. 'Get on the ball. *Here they come*!'

Next moment high above, labouring mightily, the armoured train breasted the ridge, trailing smoke stiffly behind it as it started to run down through the lines of firs marching down the slope like a regiment of spike-helmeted Prussian Guards.

Kerrigan grinned wickedly as he threw himself into cover so that the Kraut engineer at the controls couldn't see him. 'Get them drawers off, you gals,' he chuckled to himself, 'coz here I come, Pig Alley!'*

With a great hollow boom that echoed and re-echoed through the surrounding hills, the locomotive smashed into the initial barrier, tossing the thin pine logs into the air as if they were matchwood. For a few moments it disappeared into the cloud of dust and flying, splintered wood. Down below Kerrigan and his men of the Third Infantry, crouched tensely in their hiding places, held their breath. Had the Kraut train been derailed already. No, there it was again! It was coming on at top speed once more, heading straight for the bridge and destruction. 'Get ready, Reeves!' Kerrigan shouted to the combat engineer sergeant, as the clatter of the wheels, the thunder of pistons, the rush of steam grew ever louder. 'Ready to blow the bastard!'

'Ready, sir!' Reeves replied through gritted teeth, hands gripping the piston white at the knuckles, eyes fixed hypnotically on the train above them getting closer by the second.

Kerrigan held his breath. The locomotive was almost to the bridge now. At his side, Reeves breathed out hard. His shoulder muscles bulged beneath his thin khaki shirt. Beads of sweat dripped down his contorted face. He didn't seem to notice. The muscles rippled down his arms. His knuckles grew even whiter. The locomotive was on the bridge. There was the hollow clatter of its wheels on the rails. The steam trailed flatly behind it.

'*NOW*!' Kerrigan shrieked.

'*NOW*!' Reeves yelled in a savage animal bass. He thrust home the plunger with an almost sexual delight.

For one awesome, awful moment nothing happened.

* GI's corruption of Paris's Place Pigalle

Nothing! Kerrigan's eyes bulged from his head like those of a madman. He clenched his fists wildly. A crazy rage surged through his tense body. They had muffed it. 'The frigger is gonna. . .' – He stopped short.

Angry blue sparks were flashing the length of the bridge. Abruptly, little puffs of dark-brown smoke erupted between the girders. The bridge was beginning to oscillate, shake. Still the train ploughed on bravely. A series of small cracks, like twigs underfoot in a dry summer. The centre span shook. The shaking grew in intensity. The bridge buckled upwards. Abruptly the coaches were leaning to right at an absurd angle. A roar. The centre span slithered in a mess of wrecked and tangled girders to the Isère below.

Kerrigan sprang to his feet, face wild with excitement. All around his men did the same. There was no need for concealment now. Above them the guards' van and two rear coaches were yawing to one side, fighting off their fate, but being dragged inexorably down. Suddenly they sailed out into the void, turning over lazily in mid-air, carrying the trapped Germans with them, gathering speed by the instant now, until with a tremendous bone-jarring impact they slammed into the river. A huge water-spout shot up, reaching almost to the shattered bridge, and then they slid below the surface of the river, the only sign of their passing the great obscene bubbles of trapped air which now started to explode on the surface of the water.

Kerrigan ripped off his helmet and cried wildly, 'We've done it, boys! *We've done it*!'

All around him the excited, red-faced young men began to cheer, as above, the locomotive and the one remaining coach teetered on the edge of the broken bridge. Steam hissed from the locomotive. Its wheels chattered furiously as it attempted to escape its fate. But there was no escape this day. The coach began to sway back and forth alarmingly. The locomotive could no longer hold it. With a great metallic rending and tearing sound, the splintering of the heavy sleepers, the furious hissing of the escaping steam, the two of them were dragged over the side. With awesome, almost majestic ease, they sailed into the void. A second later they hit the water and exploded with a huge echoing roar that seemed to go on for ever. . .

Envoi

High above the wrecked bridge, von Dodenburg watched as the tiny figures of the Americans began to drift back to their vehicles, slapping each other's backs, gesticulating, shouting like a football crowd after a successful match. Obviously they suspected nothing. They had not even bothered to clamber down the steep banks of the Isère to check for evidence that their ambush attempt had been a success. For them Wotan had walked blindly into the trap and had been eliminated.

Crouched amid the parched grass and stunted pine, the grime-stained troopers grinned triumphantly at each other. They had pulled it off. Schulze's idea of jamming the throttle after they passed the first *maquis* ambush and just before they had breasted the rise, where it had been easy for them to jump off the slow-moving train, had worked like a dream. The *Amis* had fallen for their trick, hook, line and sinker; there had been witnesses enough to the end of SS Assault Regiment Wotan.

Down below they could hear the faint sound of the *Amis*' half-tracks starting up, and they could see the spurts of blue exhaust gas rippling in the heat. Slowly the first of the heavily laden vehicles began to move off up the dusty track and onto the road leading north, the driver honking his horn furiously as he tried to bull his way into the traffic-packed road.

Slowly von Dodenburg lowered his binoculars. He had seen enough. Southern France was firmly in American hands. Soon the whole of France would be cleared of Germans. The *Wehrmacht* had virtually nothing to stop that great khaki-clad mass of men and material rolling relentlessly northwards. Germany was finished in France. Soon that khaki tide would wash up against the frontiers of the Third Reich itself and then the grim life and death struggle would commence. Suddenly he thought of that first surprise meeting with Marchant, the Angel of Death in what now seemed another age: how that dark-eyed gaze had bored into him as he had rasped that old brutal slogan of the Foreign Legion, '*Marchez ou crevez*'. Abruptly von Dodenburg was seized by that same bitter energy, that same inner fire which must have consumed Marchant on that day. Impatiently he rose to his feet and stared around at the handful of survivors of that titanic struggle for southern France. 'All right,' he rasped, almost as if he were angry at the happy triumphant looks on their boyish faces, 'what in three devils' name are you grinning like apes for? Don't you damnwell know how far it is to the Homeland, eh?'

Schulze sprang to his feet, too, and aimed a kick at the ribs of the nearest trooper. '*Los*,' he commanded, 'have yer got frigging wax in yer ears, you bunch of piss-pansies! On your frigging feet!'

Awkwardly, hurriedly, the survivors in their ragged, stained uniforms sprang to their feet, shouldering their weapons, once more the elite of the elite.

Colonel von Dodenburg waited impatiently, his harshly handsome face set, hard gaze on the far mountains beyond. Finally Schulze swung him a tremendous salute as if he were back in the barracks in the Reich, 'SS Assault Regiment Wotan, all present and accounted for, *sir*!'

Von Dodenburg acknowledged the huge sergeant's report and salute with equal formality and rasped, 'Men, it is going to be a long walk home, with every man's hand against us. But we're going to do it, do you hear?' His hard gaze swept their youthful faces, as if challenging anyone of them to defy him. But their features remained set in hard, soldierly obedience.

Von Dodenburg nodded his silent approval and barked, '*Also los, marschieren wir*! And remember, from now on it's *MARCH OR DIE*!'

'*MARCH OR DIE*!' half a hundred hoarse young voices

took up that harsh brutal cry and then they were gone, spread out in single file, worming their way up the ever-steepening track, heading for the high mountains and the Homeland beyond. . .

SLAUGHTER AT SALERNO
Wotan 20

Leo Kessler

The Vulture gave the assembled officers one of his crooked, perverted smiles. 'The Tommies' prime objective must be the seizure of Montecorvino. I propose to take that town first.'

For Colonel Geier, the Vulture, the arrival of British troops at Salerno is another chance – maybe his last – to win the coveted general's stars. And he determines to make it his own personal Dunkirk.

But it is now September 1943. British morale is high, whereas three-quarters of his own troops are untried greenbeaks fresh from German cadet school. And following Mussolini's disappearance who knows which way the Italians will swing . . .

Futura Publications
Fiction/War
0 7088 2660 1

SCHIRMER'S DEATH LEGION
Wotan 18

Leo Kessler

'Blow the bugle, beat the drum,
Clear the streets, here comes Wo-tan . . .'

They were the *boche*, Mercier's *boche*, recruited into the Foreign Legion from the teeming POW camps in the defeated Germany of 1945. SS men, they were branded as criminals, with no future save death.

For ten years Colonel Schirmer's feared Headhunter battalion had fought in the steaming jungles of Indo-China. Now they had been brought to Algeria. For if anyone could stop the new rebellion which had just erupted there – Schirmer's Headhunters could . . .

Futura Publications
Fiction/War
0 7088 2246 0

HELLFIRE
Wotan 13

Leo Kessler

World War II is almost at an end. SS Colonel Schirmer's élite hunting commando has seen its last skirmish. But, for some, the fighting will never stop – and Schirmer has no place to hide.

Swept into the burning desert battlefields of French North Africa, he is forced to join the Foreign Legion. But first, with the shattered remnants of Assault Regiment Wotan, he must carry out one final, extraordinary raid behind Russian lines. And then learn to march – or die . . .

Futura Publications
Fiction/War
0 7088 1391 7